D0396802

CRUCIFIXION RIVER

Center Point Large Print

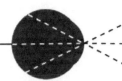

**This Large Print Book carries the
Seal of Approval of N.A.V.H.**

CRUCIFIXION RIVER

WESTERN STORIES

Marcia Muller
Bill Pronzini

CENTER POINT LARGE PRINT
THORNDIKE, MAINE

This Center Point Large Print edition
is published in the year 2012 by arrangement with
Golden West Literary Agency.

The text of this Large Print edition is unabridged.
In other aspects, this book may vary
from the original edition.
Printed in the United States of America
on permanent paper.
Set in 16-point Times New Roman type.

ISBN: 978-1-61173-282-5

Library of Congress Cataloging-in-Publication Data

Muller, Marcia.
Crucifixion river : western stories / Marcia Muller and Bill Pronzini.
p. cm.
ISBN 978-1-61173-282-5 (library binding : alk. paper)
1. Western stories. 2. Large type books. I. Pronzini, Bill. II. Title.
PS3563.U397C78 2012
813'.54—dc22
2011036249

CRUCIFIXION RIVER

WESTERN STORIES

CONTENTS

CRUCIFIXION RIVER

by Marcia Muller
and Bill Pronzini

T.J. MURDOCK

Bad storm making up. And moving in much faster than I'd expected.

You could tell it from the bruised look of the southwestern sky, the black-bellied cloud masses, the raw whip of the November wind. Already the muddy brown water of Twelve-Mile Slough—Crucifixion Slough to the locals—had roughened, creating wavelets that broke high against the muddy banks. The ferry barge, halfway across now, rocked and strained against the bridle looped over the taut guide cable. It took nearly all the strength I possessed to keep the windlass turning. If the storm broke with as much fury as I suspected it would, the crossing would be impassable well before nightfall.

The coming blow was a concern in more ways than one. Annabelle should have returned from River Bend an hour or more past. I hadn't wanted her to go at all, but she had convinced Sophie to let her take the buckboard in for supplies. Seventeen now, no longer a child but not yet old enough to find her own way in the world. Headstrong, impulsive, chafing at the isolation of our lives here at the ferry and roadhouse. The trouble in Chicago was too many years ago for her to remember it clearly, and to her there was no longer any danger or any need for hiding. Perhaps she was right. But neither Sophie nor I believed it. Patrick Bellright had a long memory, and his hate for me would surely continue to burn hotly until the last breath left his body.

On the barge, the Fosters were having difficulty with the nervous mare hitched to their farm wagon. Harlan Foster waved an arm, asking me to hurry, but it couldn't be done. The windlass creaked and groaned as it was, and the cable made sounds like a plucked banjo string as the barge inched along. At the rear of the Fosters' wagon, Sophie stood, spraddle-legged, against the pitch and sway. It was days like this one that I worried most about her assisting with the ferry work. She was as capable as any man, but cables had been known to snap and ferries to capsize, passengers and crew alike to drown. We could not afford to hire a man for the job, and, even if we could, I was loath to take the risk of it. We had been safe here for eight years now, but safety is illusory. People are seldom completely safe no matter where they are. And fugitives from a madman . . . never.

The barge was nearing the Middle Island shore. Sophie signaled and made her way forward to lower the landing apron and attend to the mooring ropes. At her next signal, I locked the windlass and straightened, flexing the aching muscles across my back and shoulders. As Sophie tied the lines and the Fosters led their skittish mare off the barge, I turned to look up along the levee road. It was still empty, although the Sacramento stage was due from River Bend any time. But the stage was not what I was looking for.

What was keeping Annabelle?

Worry, worry. About the girl, about Sophie, about Patrick Bellright, about strangers, about the weather, about a hundred other things day after day. At times it seemed our lives were nothing but a plague of worry, leavened only occasionally by hopes and pleasures. If it weren't for Sophie and Annabelle, and my writing, my life would be intolerably barren.

The wind gusted sharply, shushing in the cattails and blackerry vines and rattling the branches of the willows lining the slough. I could hear the clatter of the loose shingle on the roadhouse roof. I had been meaning to fix that, just one of the many chores that needed doing. The roadhouse, built of weathered boards reinforced with slabs of sheet metal, stood on solid ground and was solid enough itself, but the puncheon floor inside was warped in places and in need of new boards; there was painting to be done, and a new wood stove was fast becoming a necessity. Outside, the short wharf that extended into the brown water tested rickety and at least two of the pilings should be replaced. The livery barn was in good repair, except for the badly hung door and gaps in the south wall boarding.

And now winter was nigh. Another rainy season like the last would keep repair work down to the minimum necessary for reasonable comfort and survival.

This California delta, fifty miles inland from San Francisco where the Sacramento and San Joaquin Rivers merged, was a vast network of waterways and islands linked by ferries and a few levee roads. Its rugged beauty and fertile soil drew farmers, ranchers, fishermen, shanty boaters, Chinese laborers, loners, eccentric groups of one type and another—and not a few fleeing from justice or injustice. But it was a harsh land, too, prone to bad weather and winter flooding. As many people as it attracted, it drove out in defeat and despair. The Crucifixion River sect, for one instance.

I shifted my gaze to the southwest, back along the levee road to where the peninsula extended into the broad reach of the Sacramento River. Stands of swamp oak, sycamores, and willows hid what was left of Crucifixion River, the settlement that had been built along the tip—more than a dozen board-and-batten shacks and a metting house, crumbling now after seven years of abandoned neglect. The sect's dream of a self-contained Utopian community that embraced religion and free love had died quickly, destroyed by the harsh elements and the continual harassment of intolerant locals. I held no brief for

14

the sect's beliefs, but I understood all too well their desire to be left alone to live their lives in peace, without fear.

I remembered the day they'd arrived from Sacramento, three score men and women and a handful of children in a procession of wagons. Everyone had been singing, their voices raised high and joyous:

> *We shall gather at the ri-ver,*
> *the beautiful, the beautiful ri-i-ver . . .*

I remembered the day they had left, too, less than two years later. That day there had been no singing. As I ferried them across the slough, the faces aboard the wagons were bleak and stoic against a cold gray sky. I wondered again, as I had many times, what had happened to them, if they'd found their Utopia elsewhere. I hoped they had.

The Fosters and their wagon were off-loaded now and I could see Sophie waving as they clattered up to the Middle Island levee road. She threw off the mooring lines, raised and secured the apron. Even before she signaled, I had bent again to the windlass. The barge would be waiting here on the eastern shore when the stage arrived.

By the time Sophie and I had it moored tightly to the shore, the first drops of rain had begun to fall. The roiling clouds had moved closer, their underbellies black and swollen, and the wind was a howling thing that lashed the slough water to a muddy swirl. The air had an electric quality, sharp with the smell of ozone.

Sophie rubbed a hand across her thin, weathered face. "What's keeping Annabelle? She should have been home long ago."

"Some sort of delay in River Bend," I said. "No cause for concern."

"The storm is almost here."

"If she hasn't left by now, she knows to wait it out in town."

"She won't. She hates River Bend more than she does this place."

"Then she'll be here before the worst of it."

"If she isn't, how will we know she's safe?"

"The stage is due any time. Pete Dell can tell us if he's seen her."

"And if he hasn't? What then?"

We were both thinking the same. River Bend was more than a dozen miles distant and the levee road would soon enough be a quagmire. If the downpour came fast and heavy and lasted long enough, the levees might give way at some point and render it impassable. More than one traveler had been stranded, more than one conveyance swept away in the turbulent waters.

"Thomas . . . maybe I should saddle Jenny and ride toward town. . . ."

"No. If she's not back soon, I'll go."

There was more rain now, the drops blown, sharp and stinging, by the wind. I took Sophie's arm and hurried us both to the shelter of the roadhouse.

CAROLINE DEVANE

I heard the rain begin when the coach had traveled only a few miles from River Bend. The threatening storm had been a topic of conversation between the driver and station agent in River Bend, but they had decided to continue on schedule in spite of it. I unbuttoned the side curtain to note that the sky was now dark with heavy, gray clouds. It was cold and damp in the coach. Perhaps we should have remained in town.

When I rebuttoned the curtain, I saw the young man and woman on the seat opposite me looking at each other, their eyes full of concern. "What if the storm prevents us from crossing to Middle Island?" she asked him in a voice barely above a whisper.

"We'll get across." His tone wasn't reassuring, however. He was as tense as the woman, who had clasped her gloved fingers together and held her hands under her chin in an attitude of prayer.

"I wish we could have taken the steamer," she told him.

"You know why we couldn't."

They both lapsed into silence as the wind and rain buffeted the coach, causing it to rock heavily in its thoroughbraces. The storm was now full-born.

I felt some unease myself. Clinging Carrie, my brothers and sisters had called me as a child. But as an adult woman I had sinned, suffered, and lost so much that it would take far more than a storm to unnerve me.

Time passed slowly, it seemed. It was impossible to read or crochet in the jolting coach, so I studied the man and woman on the opposite seat. He was handsome in a raw-boned, strong-featured way; locks of brown hair that matched his mustache crept out from under his hat. She might have been beautiful, with her upswept auburn hair and large blue eyes and full lips, but her face showed lines of strain and dark circles underscored the eyes' loveliness. She had a prosperous look while her companion, although dressed well enough, had the weathered features and work-roughened hands of a ranch hand.

When they'd boarded the coach at the delta town of Isleton, I'd been disappointed that I was to have companions. I had taken the stage from Sacramento, rather than the river steamer, because I wished to be alone. I was starting a new life, and I needed time to prepare myself.

I had overcome my unhappiness at their presence, however, and introduced myself. After some hesitation the woman had said that her name was Rachel Kraft. "And this is my . . . cousin, Mister Hoover."

That hesitation in Rachel Kraft's voice had told me a great deal: the man was not her cousin. But what affair was that of mine? We were merely fellow passengers.

I closed my eyes, trying to picture the ranch in San Joaquin County where my sister Mary lived with her husband and seven children. Mine would be a Spartan existence there, filled with hard work—very different from the comfortable life I had enjoyed in Sacramento. But that life with my husband John and my two sons was over now; I was being thrust into exile. I knew neither Mary nor her husband Benjamin wanted me. They were only offering me shelter because I had nowhere else to go.

Fallen woman, divorced woman, shunned woman. Woman deprived of her children. Who would want such a creature?

Hugh had, in the beginning. Hugh Branson, the lover I'd taken in my unhappiness, and cherished, and eventually found wanting. After my husband discovered our affair, the fabric of my life was torn asunder. My children were taken from me in the divorce proceedings, my former friends and acquaintances turned their backs to me, and

Hugh—I'd lost Hugh as well. I'd tried to find work—I had some medical training—but word of my transgression had spread and no respectable physician or nurses' service would have me. Life in Sacramento became unbearable. The only solution was to leave. . . .

The coach lurched and slid on the levee road, which by now must have been slicked with mud. Rachel Kraft cried out and clasped Mr. Hoover's arm. The driver shouted to the horses, a sound barely audible above the voice of the wind, and the stage steadied. Mr. Hoover patted Rachel Kraft's hand, and said: "Don't fret. We'll be all right."

"If there's an accident . . ."

"There won't be an accident."

"The storm's getting worse. What if we can't cross on the ferry . . . ?"

"Hush up." It was a command, not a soothing phrase.

The coach lurched once more, and Rachel Kraft stifled a cry. Her companion comforted her as he had before, then cast an oddly guilty glance at me. There was something wrong with the pair, I thought. She panicked at the slightest provocation, and he wavered between solicitousness and tense distraction.

I closed my eyes again. My fellow passengers' troubles were of no concern to me, as mine were of no concern to them. Except for their sake and that of the driver, I would not have cared if we were cast into the slough and drowned.

Fallen woman, divorced woman, shunned woman. Woman deprived of her children.

It would have been a fitting fate.

JAMES SHOCK

An hour after I was ejected from River Bend, the skies opened wide and it began to rain like billy-be-damned. Well, it had been that type of day. A slip of the hand, an angry citizen crying— "Cheat!"—a hard-hearted sheriff, and here I was, out on the lonely road again in the midst of a storm. Instead of a dry livery and a warm meal in that swamp town's only eating house, Nell and I were forced to weather the weather, as it were— where and under what precarious conditions we'd yet to find out. Pity the poor traveling merchant!

The rain came busting down in side-slanting sheets, finding its way inside my slicker and chilling me to the marrow. Late afternoon and the sky was black as sin and the daylight all but blotted out by the deluge. The wagon lurched as Nell slogged on. Careful driving from now on, I reminded myself, to forestall an accidental plunge down the embankment to certain death. On both sides of the levee road, slough water boiled and bubbled up over the banks like soup in a witches' cauldron. If the storm grew much worse, the road would be swamped. It wouldn't do to be stranded out here at the mercy of the elements.

My luck had been running fine until River Bend and the sharp-eyed citizen and that hard-nosed sheriff. There were store boats plying this delta country, but not so many that a wagon seller couldn't make a decent living for himself. Farmers and their wives in need of clasp knives and pocket watches, writing paper and bottles of ink, saddle blankets, good maguey rope, bottles of liniment and cough syrup and female complaint medicine, needles and thread, pots and pans, spices and seasonings, yards of calico and gingham. Town citizens, too, eager to buy when their local mercantiles ran out of the goods I carried in this old red and green, slab-sided wagon with the fresh-painted words on each side:

James Shock—Fine Wares, Patent Medicines,
Knives Sharpened Free of Charge

And here and there, now and then, a few dollars to be promoted by other means. Yes, and a lonely wife or a comely young miss with a yearning for sachets and perfumes and silver Indian jewlery, and an eye for a bold young banjo-strumming traveling man.

Oh, it was a good life most of the time. Freedom. New places and new sights, and seldom the same ones twice. Even a touch of danger, and not only from the elements. For an itinerant merchant was prey to thieves who sought his money and penniless scoundrels who attempted to pilfer his wares. Not that any of them had ever succeeded in relieving Ben Shock's son of what belonged to him, no siree. The nickel-plated revolver I carried under my coat, and the Greener loaded with shells of ounce-and-a-half shot beneath the wagon seat, had seen their share of action since I inherited the wagon from my old man six years ago. And would again, I had no doubt.

The wagon bucked and skidded again, and I drew hard on the reins and braced myself on the rain-slick seat. "Steady, Nell!" I called out to the old dappled gray. She'd been a fine horse in her day, but that day was nearly past. I would have to replace her soon, before she fell over dead in the trace—as the old man had fallen over dead while mixing up a batch of worm medicine that afternoon in Carson City. It was a sad thing to watch animals and folks grow old. I was glad to be young and hale. Yes, and, if I had my druthers, that was how I would die.

But not today, and not from the fury of a gullywasher.

I seemed to recall a roadhouse and a ferry crossing somewhere along this road. But how much distance away escaped my memory. Not too far, else the Sacramento stage would have remained in River Bend instead of pulling out shortly before my own departure. Even now, it couldn't be more than half an hour ahead.

The wind blew up stronger, lashed my face with stinging wet. I ducked my head and wiped my cheeks. Smooth, hairless cheeks they were—I'd yet to need to shave them more than once a week. Baby face. More times than I could count I'd been referred to by that name, and pleased to hear it. A baby face was an asset in both business and romance. Many a customer and many a lass had succumbed to my looks and the shy manner I had learned to adopt.

Thought of lasses past and lasses to come brought a smile and a brightening of my mood. Naturally optimistic fellow, that's me, always looking on the bright side. Survival was a given in any troublesome situation, after all, and this one no different than any other. A minor setback in River Bend, a minor setback on the open road. Never fear! Providence had served me well and would continue to do so.

And it did, not more than twenty minutes later.

By then the downpour was torrential. I could scarcely see more than a few rods past the mare's nose and the road was nearly awash. The wagon slewed around a bend in the road, and there, by grab, was salvation dead ahead.

Roadhouse, livery barn, ferry barge. And beyond

the wide slough, all but hidden now by rain and misty cloud, a continuation of the road that would lead, eventually, to Stockton and points south. Ah, but not this night. Not for Nell and me, and not for the driver and passengers in the Concord coach drawn up before the roadhouse. There would be no crossings until the frenzy of the storm abated and the slough waters calmed. I had been on enough delta ferries to determine that from the look of the wind-lashed slough waters and the cable strung above them.

Well, no matter. Sanctuary from the storm was the important thing—a dry stall and hay for Nell, a warm fire and hot food for Ben Shock's son. Heigh-ho! There might even be a dollar or three to be made from the ferryman's family and the stage passengers.

ANNABELLE MURDOCK

I leaned against the buckboard, blinking away angry tears and saying words no young lady should utter.

Lady? I thought bitterly. When had I had an opportunity to learn and polish lady-like skills in this god-forsaken delta? Now it might even be the death of me. At seventeen, before I'd ever have the chance to experience all the good things life had to offer in such places as San Francisco.

I'd tarried late at the River Bend general store,

25

lingering over fancy dress fabrics that I couldn't buy and might never wear, reluctant as always to return to Crucifixion Crossing. The storm had come more quickly than anybody'd expected, and by the time I left town, the rain had started. Now it was pouring down something fierce. And as if that wasn't bad enough, a few minutes ago the front wheel hub had loosened and then jammed and the wheel had nearly come off. The spindle nut was jammed so tightly I couldn't loosen it with the wrench from the toolbox. If no one came along soon, I'd have no choice but to walk home—more than five miles, with the storm worsening by the minute.

I raised my arms to the sky and shouted: "I hate it here! I *hate* my life!" Maudie, our tired old bay mare, turned her wet head and gave me a sorrowful look. "I hate you, too!" I yelled at her. And then I burst out crying.

I was still sobbing, beating on the nut with the wrench like a demented person, when the man on horseback appeared around the bend behind me. Rescued! I was never so glad to see anybody in my life, even if he was a complete stranger.

He reined up and called out: "Miss? Are you all right?"

"Yes. It's the wheel." I banged on the hub again. "I can't get the spindle nut free to tighten it."

"Let me see what I can do." Quickly he

dismounted and came up next to me to have a look. "If you'll let me have that wrench, I think I can do the job."

And he did. In less than ten minutes he had the nut tight again so the wheel no longer wobbled. I smiled at him, my best smile. He was a good-looking man with a bushy mustache and bright blue eyes. And he had nice manners, almost courtly. Old, though. Older than Dad. He must have been at least forty. His name, he said, was Boone Nesbitt.

I told him mine and said: "I can't thank you enough for your help, Mister Nesbitt."

"My pleasure. We're both heading in the same direction, Miss Murdock. Would you mind if I rode along with you? That wheel should hold, but in this weather . . ."

"I'd be grateful if you would."

He tied his piebald horse to the buckboard and climbed up next to me on the seat. I let him take the reins. Usually I can do anything a man can, even work the ferry winch, but I was wet and miserable, and, if he wanted to drive, I was more than willing to let him.

"You live at Twelve-Mile Slough, is that right?" he asked after we were under way.

"How'd you know?"

"The storekeeper in River Bend. He's a talkative gent."

"What else did he tell you?"

27

"That your father is ferrymaster there. T.J. Murdock."

"That's right."

"The same T.J. Murdock who writes sketches and articles for San Francisco newspapers and magazines?"

"You mean you've read some of them?" I was surprised. My father's little pieces didn't pay very much or bring much attention, but he enjoyed writing them. More than I enjoyed reading them, although I pretended to him that I thought they were wonderful.

"Several," Mr. Nesbitt said. "I remember one in particular, about the religious community that once established itself nearby. Crucifixion River, it was called."

"Yes. People around here call our crossing Crucifixion instead of Twelve-Mile, and I wish they didn't."

"Why is that?"

"We never had anything to do with those people. And now that they're long gone . . . it's really a hateful place."

"Their settlement, you mean?"

"Ghost camp. No one goes there any more."

"How long have you and your family operated the ferry?"

"Oh . . . a long time. I was a little girl when we came to the delta."

"Came from where?"

I remembered Dad's warning about saying too much to anyone about our past. "*Um* . . . Kansas."

"Do you like it here, Miss Murdock?"

"No, I hate it."

"Why is that?"

"I have no friends and there's nothing to do except help with the ferry and read and sew and do chores."

"No school chums?"

"The nearest good school is in Isleton. My mother schooled me at home, but that's done now. I'm grown up. And before long I'm going away to where there are people, gaiety, excitement."

"And where would that be?"

"San Francisco, to begin with."

"I live in San Francisco," he said.

"Do you? Truly? What's it like there?"

"Not as wonderful as you might think."

Well, I didn't believe that. He was old, so his view of the city was bound to be different from mine. "I'll find out for myself one day soon," I said. "Where are you bound, Mister Nesbitt? Stockton?"

"No. Not that far."

"Are you a drummer?"

He laughed, guiding Maudie through a potholed section of the levee road. The rain was really coming down now and I was soaked to the skin. I wondered if I'd ever be warm again.

"No. I have business in the area."

"What kind of business, if you don't mind my asking?"

"I'd rather not say. It's of a personal nature."

"Well, I'm glad you came along when you did. I was just about to start walking and that can be more dangerous than riding. If there's a break in one of the levees . . . but there won't be, not unless the storm gets really bad. The only thing is, I don't think Dad will be able to operate the ferry . . . probably not until morning. You'll have to spend the night with us, Mister Nesbitt. I hope you won't mind."

"No, I won't mind," he said, solemn now for some reason. "I won't mind at all."

JOE HOOVER

When Rachel found it was storming too hard for the ferry to run, I had a hell of a time keeping her calmed down. The ferryman, Murdock, and the stage driver were huddled up under the front overhang of the roadhouse and the Devane woman had gone inside with Mrs. Murdock. Rachel wanted to get out of the coach, but I wouldn't let her do it yet. I was afraid she'd do something wild, maybe go running off like a spooked horse, if I didn't keep her close.

"We can't stay here tonight, Joe. We can't . . . we can't!"

"Nothing else we can do. Keep your head, for God's sake."

"He'll find us. He's out looking by now, you know he is. . . ."

"He won't find us."

"He will. You don't know Luke like I do. It's bad enough for his woman to run off, but the money . . ."

"Keep still about the money." I could feel the weight of it in the buckskin pouch at my belt—more than $3,000 in greenbacks and gold specie. More money than I'd ever seen or was likely to see in my life. It scared me to have it, but what scared me more was wanting to keep it.

"I shouldn't have taken it," Rachel said.

"No, you shouldn't. If I'd known what you were going to do . . ."

"I didn't plan it, I just . . . did it, that's all. We wouldn't get far without money and you don't have any of your own."

"Don't throw that in my face. Can I help it if I'm nothing more than a cowhand?"

"I didn't mean it that way, I just meant . . . oh, God, I don't know what I meant. I'm scared, Joe."

"Hold onto your nerve. We'll be all right."

"If he finds us, he'll kill us."

I didn't say anything.

"We shouldn't have left the horses in Isleton, taken the stage. If we'd kept riding, we'd be on

31

Middle Island by now, we'd be on the steamer to San Francisco. . . ."

She broke off, gasping, as the stage door popped open. It was only Murdock. Rachel twisted away from me, but if Murdock noticed how closely we'd been sitting, he didn't let on. All he said was: "Better come inside, folks."

Rachel said with the scare plain in her voice: "Isn't there any way we can cross? If there's a lull . . . ?"

"I'm afraid not. If it keeps storming this hard, you'll likely have to spend the night here."

To stop her from saying anything more, I crowded her off the seat. Murdock helped her down. She let out a little cry when he took her arm—he must've grabbed hold in one of the places she was bruised.

The stage driver called out: "Somebody coming, Murdock!"

He wheeled around. I was out of the coach by then and I peered up at the levee road. It was like trying to look through a thick silver curtain, but I could make out the shape of a big slab-sided wagon with a single horse in the trace.

"That's not Annabelle," Murdock said. He sounded worried.

"Peddler's wagon, looks like," the stage driver said.

I quit paying attention. If Luke Kraft showed, it'd be on horseback, not in a wagon. And if he did come, what then? I guessed I'd find out how much I cared for Rachel and how much I wanted that $3,000—and what kind of man I was when push came to shove.

I took Rachel's arm and we ran across to the roadhouse. It was only a few yards but we were both wet when we got inside. Worst storm I'd seen since I drifted up to the delta from Stockton three years ago. And it couldn't've come at a worse time.

I kept thinking we should've waited, made a plan, instead of running off the way we had. But Rachel couldn't stand any more of Kraft's abuse, and, truth was, I hadn't been so sure I'd go through with it if we didn't do it right away. I loved her, right enough, but Luke Kraft was the man I worked for, an important man in this country—big ranch, plenty of influence—and he had a mean streak in him wide as a mother lode. He'd come after us surely, or hire men to do it. Crazy to get myself jammed up this way over a woman. Only I couldn't help it. Once I saw those bruises, once she let me do more than look at them on her body, I was a goner. And now I was in too deep to back out even if I was of a mind to.

We stood just inside the door, dripping. The common room was big and warm, storm shutters up across its front windows. There was a food and liquor buffet on one side, a long trestle table and chairs on the other, and some pieces of horsehide furniture grouped in front of the blaze in a big stone fireplace. There wouldn't be more than a couple of guest bedrooms in back, and those for the women, so this was likely where we'd ride out the storm. Well, I'd spent nights in worse places in my twenty-four years.

The room's heat felt good after the long, cold stage ride. Mrs. Murdock fetched us towels and mugs of hot coffee. The Devane woman was sitting in one of the chairs, drying herself. I got Rachel down in the chair next to her, close to the fire. She still moved stiffly, sore from Kraft's last beating, and the other two women noticed it. I could see them wondering. The Devane woman had figured out Rachel and me were more than cousins—I'd seen it in her face on the stage. The look she gave me now was sharp enough to cut a fence post in two. I tried to tell her with my eyes and face that she was slicing up the wrong man, but she looked the other way. *Troubles of her own, that one,* I thought.

She wasn't the only one. Mrs. Murdock came in, crossed to the window next to the door, pulled the muslin aside, and looked out. The tight set of her face said she was fretting about something, but it wasn't the same kind of scare that was in Rachel.

Nobody had much to say until the door opened a few minutes later and the wind blew Murdock in. With him was a tall, smiley bird in a black slicker. When he unbuttoned it, I saw that he had a banjo slung underneath. That didn't make me like him any better. If there's one thing I can't abide, it's banjo playing.

Mrs. Murdock had come hurrying over. "Thomas . . ."

"It's all right," he said. "She's coming. I just spied the wagon."

"Oh, thank God!"

"Our daughter," Murdock said to the rest of us. "Late getting back from River Bend."

His wife threw on oilskins and the two of them hurried out into the storm. The smiley bird moved over by the fire. He had a rake's eye for a pretty face and a well-turned ankle—I could see that in the bold way he sized up Rachel and the Devane woman. I didn't like the way he looked at Rachel. Hell, I hadn't liked the look of him the second I laid eyes on him.

He introduced himself in an oily voice. "James Shock. Fine wares, patent medicines, knives sharpened free of charge."

"Peddler," I said.

"Traveling merchant, brother, if you please. At your service, Mister . . . ?"

"Hoover. Save your pitch. I'm not buying."

"Perhaps one of the ladies . . . ?"

Neither Rachel nor the Devane woman paid him any mind.

He shrugged, still smiley. I could feel the weight of that money as I sat down next to Rachel. She laid her hand on my arm and I let her keep it there; the hell with what any of the others thought.

Outside, the wind yammered and rattled boards and metal and whistled in the chimney flue. The rain on the roof made a continuous thundering sound, like a train in a tunnel. I didn't mind it so much now. I figured the longer it kept up like that, the safer we were. Not even that son-of-a-bitch, Luke Kraft, was going anywhere far in a storm like this one.

RACHEL KRAFT

There was a hot fire in the fireplace, but I couldn't get warm. My teeth chattered and I shivered and clutched Joe's arm tighter. Mrs. Murdock had brought a mug of coffee, but there was a roiling in the pit of my stomach that wouldn't permit me to drink it.

The common room was well lighted by oil lamps and candles in wall sconces, but it still seemed full of shadows. Puffs of ash drifted out of the fireplace whenever the wind blew down its chimney. After my outburst to Joe when we arrived, I could barely speak; my throat felt as if it were rusted. I looked around, wishing we were somewhere else far away and wondered what I had gotten myself into. Then I fingered the bruise on my collar bone, another on my arm, and reminded myself of what I was getting *out* of.

I didn't like the way that peddler, Shock, was looking at me, a bold stare that made me feel as though he were picturing what I looked like without my clothing. But then, he was looking at Caroline Devane in the same way. I dismissed him as the type of conceited man who viewed women—all women—as potential conquests.

Outside the wind howled, and from somewhere close by I heard a dripping sound. Probably the roof of this ramshackle old building leaked. Now that we were inside I didn't mind the storm so much, because I hoped—prayed to God—that, if Luke was already looking for us, the weather would force him to take shelter, keep him away from here until we could cross to Middle Island. But by now Luke would have discovered that the $3,000 was gone, and, if there was anything that angered him and made him determined to exact revenge, it was having his possessions taken from him. His money and his wife—in that order.

I shifted a little on the chair, and the pain in my ribs made me wince. Out of the corner of my eye I saw that Caroline Devane had noticed. She had a keen eye, had seen that I moved stiffly, and guessed the truth. She'd been giving Joe hard looks, and I wanted to cry out that it wasn't him, it was cold, hard, unyielding Luke Kraft, and, if he found us, he would kill us.

Luke. My husband. A monster. Sweet before and after our marriage until two years had passed and

I'd produced no son for him. No daughter, either, but that didn't matter. Big Luke Kraft, lord of 2,000 acres of prime delta ranch land, had an infertile wife and no son to inherit his empire. And in his anger he beat me, once broke my arm, another time tore out a patch of my hair and laughed about it, saying that it was just like scalping a damned Indian.

Thinking of him made me shiver again. Joe didn't notice. He kept his eyes on the fire, thinking Lord knew what. I knew he was angry with me for stealing Luke's money, but I also sensed that he wanted those $3,000. More than he wanted me? Oh, God, not more than me!

Remain calm, Rachel. That's what Joe's always telling you. Remain calm.

I glanced at him. In profile, he looked strong, his jaw set, his eyes focused. A man who had battled the elements working cattle ranches in Montana before he came to California. A man who was everything Luke was not—strong, gentle, kind. And unafraid of the storm raging outside.

But was he unafraid of the man whose wife he'd run off with? Would he stand up to Luke if he found us?

Of course he would. He loved me. Or kept telling me he did.

But did I love him? Or was I with him only because he was my way out of an intolerable situation?

Well, I hadn't had any choice, had I? In time Luke would have killed me, I was sure of that. I couldn't leave by myself, a woman alone with nothing and no one to rely on for protection. I'd been so sheltered as a child in Isleton, and then so isolated on Luke's big ranch, that I knew very little of the world beyond its borders.

The wind gusted, rattling what were probably loose shingles on the roof. With it came another battering downpour and a clap of thunder.

Joe gently removed my hand from his arm, favored me with one of his reassuring smiles, and stood. He moved to the buffet, poured himself a small glass of whiskey, and went to sit alone at the long trestle table.

Dear God, what if he was tiring of me? He'd been so angry with my nervous babbling when we'd first arrived here. "Keep still about the money," he'd told me. *Keep still.* He'd never spoken to me that harshly before.

The door opened, and Mrs. Murdock and a young girl of perhaps seventeen wearing mud-spattered oilskins came inside. This must be the daughter she'd been so worried about. Mrs. Murdock clucked over her like a mother hen, helped her out of the sodden rain gear, and then bustled her through the common room to the rear. I felt the dampness on the hem of my traveling skirt, and again I shivered in spite of the stove's heat.

Caroline Devane touched my arm. "There's

nothing to be concerned about," she said. "By tomorrow morning we'll be on our way."

"I wish I could believe that."

"What on earth would stop us?"

"That there's nothing to be concerned about, I meant."

After a pause the Devane woman said: "Please don't mind my saying this, but I have the feeling you're fleeing from something. You and your . . . cousin. If you'd care to confide in me . . ."

". . . I can't."

"Perhaps you wouldn't be so frightened if you did."

I've been afraid for years. Sometimes I think I'll always be afraid.

Caroline Devane put her hand on mine. Normally I don't like to be touched by strangers, but this time I didn't pull away. "We share a common bond," she said softly. "I'm running away, too, you see."

Her words surprised me. There was a quiet strength about her; she didn't seem the type to run from anything.

"Sometimes, Miss Kraft, sharing one's troubles can be a comfort to both parties."

"It's Missus Kraft," I said, and watched knowledge mixed with sorrow come into her eyes. Perhaps her troubles and mine were not so different. Perhaps we did have a common bond, that of sisters who had been badly used by the men they thought they could trust.

BOONE NESBITT

After Murdock's wife took young Annabelle inside the roadhouse, he thanked me again for helping her. I said the pleasure was all mine, and it was true in more than one sense. What she'd told me on the way confirmed my suspicions. Now it was time to prod Murdock and gauge his reaction.

When he offered to put my horse up in the barn, I said: "I'll come along and give you a hand."

"Lot drier and warmer inside, Mister Nesbitt."

"I don't mind helping out."

"Suit yourself."

He climbed up on the buckboard seat and I followed along on foot, leading the piebald I'd hired in Sacramento. Stage or steamer passage would have been more comfortable, but I prefer my own company in situations such as this. There'd be plenty of time for comfort and pleasure later on.

Thunder rumbled, loud, and jagged forks of lightning seemed to split the black sky in two. The time was not much past 4:00 p.m., but daylight was already gone and the wind-whipped rain seemed thick as gumbo. If it weren't for the lightning flares, I wouldn't have been able to see the barn until we were right up to it.

Murdock jumped down, and I helped him get

the doors propped open. A pair of hurricane lanterns flickered inside, throwing light and shadow across the Concord coach and the slab-sided peddler's wagon that took up much of the runway between the stalls. There was just enough room for the buckboard. Once he'd drawn it inside, it took both of us to drive the doors shut against the force of the storm.

Cold and damp inside, the combined smells of manure, hay, harness leather, wet animals were strong enough to make a man breathe through his mouth. A bearded oldster was busy unharnessing the stage team, putting the horses into the stalls. He paused long enough to say: "Pete Dell. Wells Fargo driver."

"Boone Nesbitt," I said.

Dell eyed my horse. "Foul weather to be out on horseback."

"That it is."

He shrugged and went on about his business. Murdock began unharnessing the wagon horse. I took my saddlebags off the piebald first, then I removed bridle and bit, uncinched the saddle, and rubbed down the horse with a burlap sack.

Murdock said conversationally: "Don't recall seeing you before, Mister Nesbitt."

"That's because I've never been in the delta before."

"You're seeing it at its worst. It's a good place to live and work most of the year."

"I prefer cities. San Francisco."

"Is that where you're from?"

"No. It's my home at present, but I'm a native of Chicago."

Murdock stiffened. His hand froze on the bay mare's halter.

"Fine city, Chicago. You ever been there, Mister Murdock?"

"No," he said. He finished unharnessing the bay without looking at me, led it into one of the remaining stalls. I ambled over next to Murdock as he measured out a portion of oats. Pete Dell was out of earshot, with the rain beating hard against the roof and walls, but I kept my voice low anyhow.

"Your daughter told me you're the T.J. Murdock who writes sketches for the San Francisco periodicals."

The look he gave me had a mask on it. "Now and then. A hobby."

"I've read some of them. Reminiscent of Ambrose Bierce, but with a distinctive style all your own. Very distinctive, as a matter of fact."

"If you think so, I'm flattered."

"The one in the *Argonaut* about the Crucifixion River sect was particularly good."

"That was several years ago," Murdock said warily.

"Yes, I know. I looked it up after I'd read some of your more recent sketches. You wrote it from first-hand knowledge, I understand."

43

"That's right. The sect established itself on the peninsula southwest of here."

"Buildings still standing?"

"Mostly."

"Ghosts. The past is full of them."

He had nothing to say to that.

"Funny thing," I said, "how the past can haunt the present. I wonder if the sect members are haunted by their failure here."

"I wouldn't know."

"I'll wager some of them are. Some folks just can't escape their past failures. Or their past sins."

A muscle jumped along his jaw. He seemed about to say something, changed his mind. The mask was back in place, tight as ever. He finished rubbing down the roan, slung a blanket over the animal, and called to Pete Dell: "Going inside now, Pete! Come on in for some hot grub when you're finished."

"I'll be there. Pour me a whiskey to go with it."

"Done. You planning to spend the night in the common room or out here?"

"Out here. Prefer my own company at night, you know that."

"It'll be pretty cold and damp. This barn's drafty."

"Warm enough for me inside the coach."

"Suit yourself." Murdock started toward the doors, glanced back at me long enough to say: "You coming, Mister Nesbitt?"

"Right behind you."

He went on with his shoulders squared, slipped out through one door half, closed it after I followed, and set off in hard strides to the roadhouse. Walking, not running. He was through running, one way or another—we both knew that now.

T.J. Murdock? Not by a damned sight. His true name was Harold P. Baxter and he was a native of Chicago, same as I was. And after eight years, purely by chance, I was the man who'd found him, I was the man who stood to collect the private reward of $10,000 on his head.

ANNABELLE MURDOCK

The common room had never seemed so alive! Two women sitting by the fire, a good-looking man with a banjo slung over his shoulder helping himself at the buffet, another fellow drinking whiskey at the table, and Mr. Nesbitt and my father and Pete Dell yet to join us. Everyone was subdued by the storm, but as glad to be out of it as I was. This much company was a rare treat; we seldom had more than two or three guests. There were only two guest bedrooms, for ladies only if the company was mixed, and it was seldom that both were occupied for a night.

I'd changed clothes in my bedroom and dried my hair as best I could. Dratted hair—when wet and damp, it curled and tangled and looked like a mare's nest. Yet another reason I hated this backcountry. At least my dress was pretty; I'd put on the blue gingham with the lace collar for our company.

I looked around at the stranded travelers. The women by the fire had their heads together in earnest conversation—stage passengers, surely. The man drinking whiskey at the table looked to be a farm or ranch worker dressed up in his Sunday best. The other man at the buffet, the one with the banjo, had his back to me, but I'd gotten a close look at him when I came in. My, he was handsome in his brown butternut suit. And much nearer to my age than Mr. Nesbitt. Mother came out and placed a basket of fresh-baked bread beside him, and he smiled and nodded his thanks before she returned to the kitchen.

The door opened and Dad came in. His face was tightened up like it got when he'd fought with me or Mother, and he moved in an odd, jerky way. He didn't even look at me as he shucked out of his oilskins and then walked through the room toward the kitchen. It made me cross. I hate to be ignored, and it was particularly annoying after the soaking I'd gotten and the wheel almost coming off the buckboard. Then Mr. Nesbitt came in, and *he* nodded to me as he took off his wet slicker.

I went to the buffet for coffee, and greeted the man with the banjo. Oh, yes, he truly was good-looking—slender, with chestnut brown hair and a nice smile and a rakish gleam in his eyes. And tall—I had to tilt my head to look up at him. I like tall men, probably because I'm short and a man half a head taller makes me feel protected.

He said, smiling: "You must be Miss Murdock."

"Yes. My name is Annabelle."

"James Shock, traveling merchant, at your service."

"Oh, is that right? Where's your wagon?"

"Safe in the barn. It contains all manner of fine merchandise, for ladies as well as men." He raised one eyebrow questioningly.

"Are you trying to sell me something, Mister Shock?"

"An attractive young woman like yourself can always use a new hat, a hair ribbon, sachets, perfume, a bolt of good cloth."

"I've no money for such things . . . not that I wouldn't love to have them."

"My prices are more reasonable than any in town stores."

"They could cost a penny each and I couldn't buy them."

"That's a shame. It truly is."

"I think so, too. May I ask how long you've been a peddler?"

"Traveling merchant, if you please. All my life. My father was in the trade before me and I learned it at his side."

"You must have seen a lot of different places."

"I have, indeed. Traveled far and wide throughout the West."

"Is that so? Have you been to San Francisco?"

"Ah, yes. Many times. I expect I'll be paying another visit before long."

"It's wonderful, isn't it? A wonderful, exciting city."

"That it is, if you know it well. And I do. You've never been there yourself?"

"No, never. The only city I've ever been to is Sacramento, with my folks." I heard myself sigh. "I'd give anything to live in San Francisco. And to visit all the other places you've seen."

He smiled more widely, showing even white teeth. "Why don't you, then?"

"I'm too young. My folks say I am anyway."

"Young, mayhap, but a woman nonetheless. A beautiful young woman."

Well, I couldn't help smiling and preening a little at such flattery. *Lovely woman. Beautiful young woman.* Mr. James Shock was a charmer, he truly was. And so easy to talk to, and to look at. The more I looked into those eyes of his, the more tingly I felt. Why, he all but gave me goosebumps.

"Tell me about your travels," I said. "Tell me about San Francisco."

"With pleasure, Annabelle. I may call you Annabelle?"

"Please do."

"And you'll call me by my given name, if you please. James . . . never Jim."

I laughed. "Will you play a song for me on your banjo, Mister James Never Jim Shock?"

He laughed, too. "That I will," he said. "As many as you like."

"Do you know 'Little Brown Jug'?"

"One of my favorite tunes." He caressed me with his eyes and I felt the goosebumps rise again. "I can see that we're going to be good friends, Annabelle. Yes, indeed. Very good friends."

T.J. MURDOCK

Supper was later than usual because of all the extra mouths to feed. After I finished eating, I donned my slicker and went outside to check on the ferry lashings and the cable. The driving rain had let up some, but the wind remained strong. I had to push my way through it, bent forward at the waist, as if it were something semi-solid.

I thought Boone Nesbitt might follow me, but he didn't. All through the meal I'd felt his eyes on me, dark and implacable in a pokerface. He hadn't said a word to me since the barn, and none to any of the others except for a brief response when someone addressed him directly. I had also remained silent. As had the other stranded travelers, except for the banjo-strumming peddler, Shock, who had kept up a running sales pitch for his various wares and told stories that Annabelle, if no one else, seemed to find entertaining. There was a lost quality to Caroline Devane, a strained tension in Joe Hoover and his companion that seemed more a product of private troubles than the pounding storm. But no one was as tautly wound as I, nor as troubled.

Nesbitt knew my real identity, there was little doubt of that from his questions and comments in the barn. A stranger from San Francisco by way of Sacramento, alone on horseback . . . come upon me so suddenly that I could scarcely think straight. Who was he? What was his game, with his sly talk and watchful eyes? Waiting for the storm to abate, likely, to make his intentions known to me. We both knew there was no escape while the storm raged, and none afterward because of Sophie and Annabelle.

How had he found me, after eight long years? My sketches in the *Argonaut*, *The Overland Monthly*, and other San Francisco publications? He had made a deliberate point of mentioning them and my distinctive writing style. I'd been a fool to submit my writings for publication, even under the Murdock name and in a city far from Chicago. But a writer such as I was and had been for the Chicago *Sentinel* is one who yearns not for fame or money, but to have his words, ideas, insights read by others. And the pittances I was paid augmented the pittance I earned as a ferrymaster, allowing us what few small luxuries we could afford.

I didn't know what to do about Nesbitt. What could I do? Even if it weren't for my family, I would not have run again. The flight from Chicago in 1887, the years of hardship since, were all of a fugitive's life I could bear. If Nesbitt was bent on taking me back to face Patrick Bellright, there seemed little choice but to submit. If he was an assassin hired to finish me here, I would try to defend myself, but I would not take action against him first. I could not premeditate the destruction of a human life, even to save my own. It simply was not in me.

The ferry barge was secure, the cable whipped taut and singing in the wind but showing no indication that it might snap. Crucifixion Slough was a cauldron, frothing near to the tops of the embankments on both shores, inundating the cattails and blackberry shrubs that grew on this side. The levee road, as far as I could tell in the darkness, had not been breached close by, but if the storm's fury continued long enough, there were bound to be breaks between here and River Bend and over on the Middle Island roads. In any case, it would be long hours through the night and perhaps into the morning before the ferry could be operated—long, difficult hours of waiting for Nesbitt to reveal himself.

I started back to the house, the wind's might

behind me now and forcing me into a lope. Before I got there, however, a pair of shapes materialized, suddenly and astonishingly, on the levee road above. Horse and rider, coming as fast as could be managed through the downpour. I stopped and rubbed wet out of my eyes, blinking. It was no trick of night vision. When the rider reached the muddy embankment lane, he swung in and slid his mount down and across the yard.

He drew rein when he spied me, veered over to where I stood, and dismounted. He wore a heavy poncho and a scarf-tied hat that rendered his face all but invisible. All I could tell about him was that he was big and that his voice was rough-toned, thickened by liquor and an emotion I took to be anger.

"My Lord, what are you doing out on such a night?"

He ignored the question. "Who're you?" he demanded.

"T.J. Murdock, ferrymaster here."

"My name's Kraft. Afternoon stage comes this way, bound for Stockton. You ferry it across before the storm broke?"

"No, it arrived too late for safe passage."

He made a hard, grunting sound. "Passengers still here, then?"

"Yes. Until morning likely."

"Rachel Kraft one of them? Woman, twenty-eight, roan-color hair braided and rolled, pretty face?"

"Yes."

"And a man with short, curly hair and a thick mustache?"

"He's here, too, yes. Is Rachel Kraft related to you?"

"Damn right she is . . . my wife. Where are they?"

"Inside with the others. Mister Kraft, why . . . ?"

He wheeled the horse, spurred it hard toward the house. I hurried after him through the muddy puddles. He jumped down, left the animal where it stood with no thought to its care, and literally ripped at the door latch. I was only a few paces behind him when he bulled his way inside the common room.

The guests were all still at table, lingering over coffee and dried apple pie, Shock picking on his banjo. Rachel Kraft's reaction to sight of her husband was to let loose a keening wail. Joe Hoover stood up fast, nearly upsetting his chair on the near side of the table. Everyone else froze. I shut the door against the rain and wind as Luke Kraft swept his hat back off his head. When I stepped around him, I had a clear look at his face and what I saw stood me dead-still. It was blotched dark red from drink, cold, and the clear mix of fury and hate that brewed inside him.

Rachel Kraft's expression was one of bloodless terror. "Oh, my God . . . Luke!"

"Didn't think I'd find you this fast, did you? You and that son-of-a-bitch you run off with."

Hoover said: "Leave her be, Kraft."

"Like hell I will. You ain't getting away with what you done. She's coming back with me, her and the money both. Right now, storm or no storm."

"You can have the money and welcome, but not Rachel."

"Shut up, Hoover. No damn' thieving wife stealer's gonna stand in my way."

"Listen to me. . . ."

Kraft swept the tail of his poncho back, snaked a hand underneath. It came out filled with a long-barreled Colt sidearm. Rachel Kraft cried out again. Nesbitt stood up, doing it slowly, with his hands in plain sight. None of the rest of us moved an inch.

"There's no call for that, Mister Kraft," I said, with as much calm as I could muster. "There are women in here."

"Only woman I'm interested in is my wife. Rachel, get on over here."

"No, Luke, please. . . ."

"I said get over here. Now!"

"She's not going back with you," Hoover said.

"You gonna stop me from taking her? Go ahead and try. I'd just as lief put a bullet in you."

54

"She's had all the beatings she can stand. I've seen the marks you put on her."

"Yeah, and I know what the two of you was doing when you seen 'em. Rachel! Do what you been told!"

She obeyed this time. Her legs were unsteady as she rose to her feet and started toward him.

Hoover stepped in front her, pushed her behind him, and held her there with one arm. His jaw was set hard. He'd struck me as mild-mannered, but there was plenty of sand and iron in him. The thought crossed my mind that he was more in love with Rachel Kraft than her husband ever could be.

"You can't have her, Kraft."

"I'm taking what's mine, all of it."

She said through her fright: "Luke, Joe didn't steal the money. I did. He didn't know anything about it until after we left. . . ."

"Shut up. I won't tell you again . . . get on over here!"

Hoover took a step forward, still holding the woman behind him. "Suppose we keep this between you and me. . . ."

Kraft shot him. Just that quickly.

The sound of the gunshot was nearly deafening in the low-ceilinged room. The bullet struck Hoover in the chest, threw him around, grunting, and down to the floor. Shocked gasps and cries rode the dying echoes of the shot. Rachel Kraft screamed, took one look at the blood streaming from Hoover's chest, and fainted.

The sudden violence, the acrid fog of powder smoke in the air, seemed to have no effect on Nesbitt. He said to Kraft: "You shot an unarmed man, mister. If he dies, that's murder."

"Bastard stole my wife and three thousand dollars out of my safe."

"That's no cause for gun play."

"You saw him start for me. Self-defense, by Christ."

"Everyone here will testify otherwise."

Kraft pointed his weapon at Nesbitt. What he'd done seemed to have had no effect on the rage and hatred that controlled him. "That's enough out of you. You and Murdock pick up my wife and carry her outside and put her on my horse. Tie her down if needs be."

I said: "Be reasonable, man. You can't take her out in this storm. . . ."

"Don't you start in on me, mister, unless you want a bullet, too. We're leaving here as soon as I . . ."

The rest of what he'd been about to say was lost in another report, not as loud but just as sudden and shocking. A bloody hole appeared in Kraft's forehead; he had time for one amazed gasp before his knees buckled and he fell headlong, his weapon coming free of his grasp. I tore my gaze away from his settling body, put it on the shaken, gabbling group around the table.

The peddler, James Shock, said: "That *was* self-defense, brothers and sisters. I trust you'll all testify to the fact."

In his hand, smoke adrift from the muzzle, was a small, nickel-plated revolver.

CAROLINE DEVANE

Mr. Nesbitt and I were the first to move after James Shock's pronouncement. He went to kneel beside the man named Kraft while I hurried to Joe Hoover's side. Young Hoover was alive, barely conscious and moaning, blood pumping from the wound in his chest. As I knelt quickly beside him, I heard Nesbitt say that the drunken rancher was dead. Others were moving about, too, by then, Mrs. Murdock attending to Rachel Kraft.

Hoover's wound, fortunately, was high on the left side of his chest, below the collar bone—a location where there were no vital organs. There was considerable blood, but it was not arterial blood. Serious, then, but perhaps not life-threatening if the bullet could be removed, the wound cleaned and properly treated to reduce the threat of infection.

Mr. Murdock said: "How badly hur is he?"

I told him my prognosis.

"Sounds like you've had nurse's training."

"I have," I said. I looked past him at his wife.

"We'll need hot water, clean towels, a sharp, clean knife. Have you any disinfectant?"

"Only rubbing alcohol."

"That'll do. Also sulphur powder, if you have that."

She nodded and hurried away.

Rachel Kraft had recovered from her faint and was sitting up, staring at us with horrified eyes. "Joe," she said. "Oh, God, don't let him die."

"He's not going to die," I said with more conviction than I felt.

She moaned, made an effort to stand, failed, and began to crawl toward us. Nesbitt grasped her arms and drew her to her feet. She cried out in protest, struggled for a moment, and suddenly went limp again. Not the sort of woman one could rely upon in a crisis such as this.

Murdock asked me: "Can he be moved?"

"Yes, I think so."

"We'll take him into one of the guest rooms."

I stood and moved aside as he and Mr. Nesbitt lifted the injured man. Nesbitt had helped Rachel Kraft to a chair by the fire; she was conscious again, but inert, and she wore the glazed look of deep shock. James Shock still stood by the table, and, as I followed the men carrying Hoover, I glanced at the peddler. He was smiling faintly, his gaze fixed and thoughtful. He didn't seem particularly affected by the fact that he had just killed a man, and it made me wonder if he had killed before. Whether he had or not, the man's coldness, his unctuousness, his conviction that all women would fall prey to his superficial charm, repelled me.

The men laid young Hoover on the guest room bed. With Mr. Murdock's help, I removed the wounded man's coat and shirt. Sophie Murdock came with towels, a bottle of rubbing alcohol, a package of sulfur powder. Laudanum, too, for pain relief afterward. "The water's heating," she said. "It won't be long."

"The knife will have to be sterilized."

"Yes. I have it in another pan on the stove."

I used a towel to sponge blood from the wound. It was as I'd surmised from my cursory examination in the common room—serious but not necessarily life-threatening. Hoover moaned and his eyelids fluttered, then popped open. Pain clouded his eyes, but he managed to focus on me.

"Rachel," he whispered.

"Lie still, Mister Hoover."

"I have to know . . . she all right?"

"Yes. Unharmed."

"Kraft?"

"He's dead," Murdock said. "The peddler, Shock, shot him."

Hoover muttered something, a sound of satisfaction, and his body relaxed and his eyes closed again.

I drew the Murdocks aside. "We'll need a bottle of whiskey," I said. "For anaesthesia. I can't probe into him unless he's partially sedated and held still."

"I'll get it," Murdock said.

"Another lamp, too. More light."

The three of them hurried out, leaving me alone with Hoover. He looked so young and vulnerable, lying there—like one of my own sons. He may have been a thief, as that man Kraft had said, but he was personable and he seemed genuinely to care for Rachel Kraft.

The Murdocks returned with the rest of the items I had requested. I positioned them, one on either side of the bed. Murdock lifted Hoover's head and administered a large dose of whiskey. I sponged more blood from the wound, cleaned it with alcohol—he groaned again but lay still—and then stood staring at the sterilized kitchen knife gleaming on a cloth beside the pan of boiled water. My hand was not steady and perspiration beaded my forehead.

Sophie Murdock looked keenly at me, her tired eyes searching mine. "You've never had cause to do this before, have you?"

"No." My voice was as unsteady as my hand.

"But you have assisted with similar procedures."

"Yes . . . once."

"Then you'll manage. Won't she, Thomas?"

"I have no doubt of it," he said.

I drew several deep breaths. Mrs. Murdock was right—I *would* manage to do what was necessary to save this young man's life. I would because I must.

My hand no longer trembled when I reached out for the knife.

JAMES SHOCK

After the wounded wife stealer was carried out, I ambled over for a look at the gent I'd shot. Drilled dead center above the bridge of the nose, by grab. Never knew what hit him. Never expected a banjo-strumming peddler to have a hide-out gun, or in the blink of an eye to draw and fire with perfect aim. He wasn't the first to suffer the consequences of underestimating James Shock, and like as not he wouldn't be the last.

As I turned away, the Murdock girl, Annabelle, came near and caught hold of my arm. Her face was bloodless, but nonetheless attractive for her fright. She wouldn't look at the dead man; her eyes were all for me. "That was a brave thing you did, Mister Shock," she said, all breathless. "Truly it was."

I smiled down at her. Her body was pressed so tightly against my arm I could feel the swell of her breasts. What a sweet little piece she was, all tender and dewy-eyed and ripe for the picking.

But not by me, alas. Not in these surroundings and under these circumstances. Underage she was, too. Jail bait. Pity.

"I couldn't let him fire his weapon a second time," I said. "He might've shot someone else . . . even *you,* my dear."

I felt her shiver and squeeze tighter, tight enough to bring a stir to my loins. Seventeen and surely a virgin. I sighed, licking my lips, and reluctantly eased her away from me. No sense in allowing such warm flesh to torment me, eh? Besides, I had more important matters on my mind. Percolating there, you might say.

Murdock and the sharp-eyed gent named Nesbitt returned from wherever they'd carried Hoover. Annabelle stepped farther away from me as Nesbitt approached. Murdock went to the buffet for a bottle of whiskey, then picked up one of the coal-oil lamps. Annabelle said to him, dipping her chin in the direction of the dead man: "Dad, will you please take . . . *that* outside. He . . . it's making me ill."

"I can't right now. Nesbitt?"

"Shock and I will do it."

I shrugged. "For the lady's sake, yes."

"We'll put him in the barn."

"All that distance in this weather? Why not just lay him out front?"

"Cold, aren't you, Shock?"

"Not at all, brother. Practical is the word. After

the way he busted in here, a raging threat to all of us, his remains don't deserve consideration."

"The barn. Come on, let's get it done."

Well, I might have argued with him, but I held my tongue. Peace and harmony, now the crisis was ended—that was the ticket. I shrugged and winked at Annabelle and went to put on my rain gear.

And out we went into the storm, my hands full of the dead rancher's scuffed boots, and across a mud field to the barn. The stage driver had gone back out there earlier to sleep in his coach and the storm had prevented him from hearing the gunfire. He woke up quickly when we came staggering in and laid the corpse in one of the empty stalls. Nesbitt gave him a terse explanation of the events inside. Dell said he'd fetch Kraft's horse and went out to do that.

On one knee, Nesbitt ran his hands over Kraft's clothing. Searching for a wallet or purse, mayhap, but he found nothing of the sort. When he stood up again, he said: "You're quite a marksman, aren't you, Shock? For an itinerant peddler."

"A man's profession has little to do with his ability with firearms."

"True enough. Still, it was pretty risky, firing as you did in there. Suppose you'd missed?"

"But I didn't miss."

"But you could have."

"Not at that range, with the element of surprise

in my favor," I said. "No, brother, the only danger was that Kraft might have had a notion to fire his weapon again, as drunk and raging as he was. I did what I had to do for all our sakes. You'd have done the same, given the opportunity."

"Would I? Why do you say that?"

"You wear a sidearm. Before I drew and fired, I saw you ease the tail of your coat back."

"Very observant. But I wouldn't have drawn unless Kraft turned his gun in the direction of the table."

"Might've been too late by then. I chose to act immediately. The right choice, eh, brother?"

"As it turned out."

He gave me a long, searching look. As if he were trying to take my measure. It was the scrutiny of a lawman, one I'd seen too many times in my life to mistake. Well, if a lawman was what he was, no matter to me or my plans. I was not wanted anywhere for any sort of crime. A few close calls here and there, that was all. And no one could dispute the fact that I'd plugged the rancher in self-defense; half a dozen witnesses could attest to that. I had nothing to fear from the law. And wouldn't after I left here, if I were careful.

On the walk back to the roadhouse, I thought again of what Luke Kraft had said after shooting down the wife stealer. *Bastard stole my wife and three thousand dollars out of my safe.* Three thousand dollars! No one other than the ever-vigilant James Shock seemed to have paid attention to those words. And where were the $3,000 to be found? In the wife's or the cowhand's luggage, possibly, but more likely it was on the cowhand himself. As he'd lain there on the floor, with the Devane woman ministering to him, I'd spied a cowhide pouch fastened to his belt. What better place to keep greenbacks or gold specie or both?

Heigh-ho! And who better to lay claim to those $3,000 than the resourceful Mr. James Shock?

ANNABELLE MURDOCK

After James Never Jim Shock and Mr. Nesbitt took the dead man away, I went over to where Mrs. Kraft slumped in a chair in front of the fireplace. Even though the room was warm, she was shaking as if she had the ague and her eyes were unfocused. Well, of course she was in bad way. She'd just seen her husband shoot her lover—*that* had been a surprise, Joe Hoover being her lover, even though the two of them hadn't really acted like cousins—and then her husband shot dead right afterward.

I was still upset myself. All that sudden violence—right here in my home! Oh, we'd had incidents before, drummers imbibing too much whiskey, men cheating at cards and getting into fights. But they'd never been anything that Dad couldn't resolve without any shooting being done. What had happened tonight had been terrible to see. I'd probably have nightmares about it for the rest of my life. If it hadn't been for James Never Jim Shock, that man Kraft might have shot his wife, too, and maybe Dad, or Mother, or even me. It made me shudder again just thinking about it.

"Missus Kraft?" I said.

She didn't answer. Didn't even look at me.

Shaking the way she was, even with the fire, she ought to have a blanket. I hurried to my room, where I stripped away the good heavy woolen one that Mother had ordered for me from a Sears Roebuck catalog last summer. When I came back into the common room, Rachel Kraft hadn't moved. I wrapped the blanket around her and sat down on the chair to her right. And this time when I spoke her name, she turned her head and looked at me with dull eyes.

"Joe," she said. "Mister Hoover. He'll live, won't he?"

I didn't know, but I said: "I think so. Missus Devane and my folks . . . they're doing all they can."

"And my husband? He's dead?"

"Yes. I'm sorry."

She looked back at the fire. "Don't be. He deserved to die. You saw and heard what kind of man he was." After a moment, she added: "A harsh man created by a harsh land. This is no

66

place to make a decent life, especially for a woman."

I nodded. That was exactly how I felt.

"Mister Hoover and I were going away together," she said. "I don't know where, just . . . away. If he dies . . ."

"He won't die."

"You don't know that he won't."

"I don't know it, but I believe it. You should, too."

"You're so young, so full of optimism. And I'm . . ."

"Not old," I said quickly. "Not much older than me."

"But I've lived a much harder life. You don't have any idea how hard."

No, I didn't. But I could imagine. From all the things that man Kraft had said before he shot Mr. Hoover, her life with him must have been awful.

"Regardless of what happens to Joe, I'm going far away from here. I hate the delta. I've always hated it."

"So have I."

"Then don't make the mistake I did," Mrs. Kraft said. "Don't stay here, don't linger a moment longer than you have to. Leave before it's too late."

As soon as she said that, I thought of James Never Jim Shock. Truth to tell, I hadn't stopped thinking about him since I'd first set eyes on him.

Such a handsome man. And he wasn't a mere peddler. He was . . . well, a sort of happy banjo-playing troubadour who'd traveled far and wide, seen wonderful places, and done all manner of exciting things. A free spirit. And a hero, too, the way he'd saved us all from harm tonight.

Did I dare let him be my way out of here?

He seemed as taken with me as I was with him. He'd called me a beautiful woman, and the touch of his hand on mine, the hard muscles I'd felt when I hugged his arm—the memory made me all tingly again, my face feel warm. He was everything I'd ever dreamed of in a man, wasn't he? And he'd be good to me, I was sure of it.

Dad. Mother. The idea of stealing away—they wouldn't let me go voluntarily, not alone and never with a man I'd only just met—and perhaps never seeing them again made me feel sad. I loved them both and their lives had been difficult since that accident in Chicago when I was a child. Mother was so tired, worn down by years of hard work, and lonely except for my company. Dad worked hard, too, his writing his only escape. It put a hollow feeling in my chest, thinking of what would become of them when I left. But I had to think of myself first, didn't I? Don't you always have to think of yourself first when you're young and trapped?

I glanced over at Mrs. Kraft. She was staring into the flames, her mouth bent down, eyes blank again. No, I wasn't going to turn out like her—beaten, broken, and, despite what she claimed, probably trapped here in the delta for the rest of her life. She wasn't a strong woman, not like my mother, not like me. If Joe Hoover didn't live, she'd be completely alone, with nowhere to go.

I went back to my room, where I lay down on my bed in the dark, pulling the quilt around me. Mrs. Kraft was right. This was no place to make a decent life. I couldn't linger here; I had to leave before it was too late. The only question was whether I should wait and make my way alone or leave right away with James Never Jim Shock.

BOONE NESBITT

I spent most of the long night sprawled in one of the overstuffed chairs near the hearth. Now and then I dozed, but I was too keyed up to sleep. Mostly I tended to the fire, listened to the wind and rain, and let my thoughts wander.

The shootings had put me on edge. Sudden violence always has that effect on me, whether I'm directly involved or not. I'd shot two men in my time, been fired upon by them and by two others, drawn sidearm and rifle on half a dozen more, and I was weary of gun play. Weary, too, of drunken fools like Luke Kraft and cold-blooded types like James Shock. No simple peddler, Shock. I'd seen his breed before: sly, deadly connivers hiding behind bright smiles and drummers' casual patter. Kraft wasn't the first man he'd killed with that hide-out weapon of his; the swift draw, the dead-aim bullet placed squarely between the rancher's eyes at forty paces, proved that. He was a dangerous man, capable of any act to feather his nest, and he knew that I knew it. Knew what I was, just as I knew what he was. He'd been as watchful of me as I'd been of him since we'd had our conversation out in the barn.

Be more to my liking if I was here after Shock instead of Harold P. Baxter, alias T.J. Murdock. Shock was the sort I'd always enjoyed tracking down and yaffling—a proper match for my skills and my dislike of criminals. Murdock, on the other hand, seemed to be a decent family man. Likable. Intelligent. Non-violent. His only sin was an incident eight years ago in Chicago, unavoidable and accidental by all accounts except one. If any man other than Patrick Bellright had been affected, Murdock and his wife and daughter wouldn't have had to flee for their lives, or to spend eight years hiding in a California backwater like this one.

Yes, and if any man other than Patrick Bellright had been affected, I wouldn't be here ready and willing to tear their patchwork lives to shreds for a $10,000 reward.

Pure luck that I'd found him. Murdock might've

lived the rest of his life at Twelve-Mile Crossing if Bellright hadn't employed the Pinkerton agency; if I hadn't been transferred from the Chicago to the San Francisco office; if I hadn't had a penchant for back-checking old, unsolved cases; if Murdock hadn't risked publishing sketches in San Francisco newspapers and magazines and I hadn't spotted the similarities to Harold P. Baxter's writings for the Chicago *Sentinel*. Circumstances had conspired against him, and in my favor. Bellright's favor, too. Patrick Bellright—financier and philanthropist, with a deserved reputation as a hater and seeker of vengeance and brass-balled son-of-a-bitch.

There wasn't much doubt what he'd do when I brought Harold P. Baxter back to Chicago to face him. He'd pay me my blood money and dismiss me, and a short time later Baxter would either turn up dead in a trumped-up accident or disappear never to be heard from again. An eye for an eye, that was Bellright's philosophy. Hell, he was capable of killing Baxter himself and laughing while he did it.

But that wasn't my look-out now, was it? I'd made my living for twenty years as a manhunter, and I'd been responsible for the deaths of several fugitives, by my own hand and by state execution. One more didn't matter. That was what I'd told myself when I set out from San Francisco two days ago. A stroke of good fortune like no other I could ever expect in my life. Ten thousand dollars. An end to twenty years of hard, violent detective work and hand-to-mouth living, a piece of land in the Valley of the Moon, maybe a woman to share it with one day. I was entitled, wasn't I?

Sure I was. Sure.

The only trouble was, now that I was here, now that I'd met Harold P. Baxter and his family, doubts had begun to creep in. He was a fugitive, yes, but not from the law and likely not in the eyes of God. All the men I'd tracked and sent to their deaths before had been guilty of serious crimes, but Baxter was an innocent victim of fate and one man's lust for revenge. Send him to a certain death and I would no longer be on the side of the righteous; I'd be a paid conspirator in a man's murder.

Ten thousand dollars. Thirty pieces of silver.

In San Francisco I'd convinced myself I'd have no trouble going through with it. Now I wasn't so certain.

I dozed for a time, woke to add another log to the fire, dozed again. When I awakened that time, I saw that James Shock was no longer asleep on the nearby sofa. A visit to the privy out back? Or was he up to something? The way he'd been making up to Annabelle hadn't set well with me; she seemed smitten with him. I wouldn't put it past him to sneak into her room. . . .

No, it was all right. Just as I was about to get up

for a look around, Shock came gliding back into the common room, paused to glance my way, and then laid down again on the sofa. Wherever he'd gone, it hadn't been to answer a call of Nature. He hadn't put on his rain gear and he was still in his stocking feet.

I sat watching the fire, listening to the rain slacken until it was only a soft patter on the roof. The storm seemed finally to be blowing itself out. I flipped open the cover on my stemwinder, and leaned over close to the fire to read the time. Some past 5:00 a.m. Be dawn soon.

And before another nightfall I'd have to make up my mind about Harold P. Baxter, one way or the other.

RACHEL KRAFT

I was still sitting in front of the fireplace, my mind mostly blank as it always used to be after one of Luke's beatings, when Sophie Murdock came through the door from the bedrooms. At sight of her, I sat up straight, an icy fear spreading through me.

"Joe? He's not . . . ?"

"No. Resting peaceably," she said. "Missus Devane removed the bullet and dressed his wound. You can see him now."

I stood haltingly, a sharp ache in my ribs where two days ago Luke had twice kicked me after knocking me to the floor, and followed the ferryman's wife to a small guest room. Joe lay on a narrow bed, his eyes closed; Caroline Devane was pulling a quilt over him. She straightened, putting a hand to the small of her back as if it ached, and turned toward me.

While Mrs. Murdock gathered up some bloody towels and a basin of pink-tinged water, Caroline said: "He'll sleep for some time, and I think he'll be all right when he wakes."

"I'm grateful for you helping him."

"I'm glad I was able to."

"Would it be all right if I sat with him?"

"Of course. I'll be in the next room. Rouse me if he wakes."

"Yes, I will."

The women left the room, and I moved toward the bed. Joe's brow was damp, his hair disheveled. In sleep, he looked more like a little boy than a grown man who had thrust himself between me and Luke's long-barreled Colt. I took my handkerchief from my skirt pocket, wiped his brow, and then drew over a rocker from the other side of the room and sat close to the bed, studying his face.

It was a good face, strong if not particularly handsome, weathered by his work on the range. He'd taken me away from the ranch, forgiven me for stealing Luke's money, and given me hope for a new and better life.

But did I love him? I'd wondered before if he were merely a way out for me. Now that I no longer needed him to defend me from Luke . . .

With a sense of shock, I realized what I hadn't allowed myself to think before. I was now a wealthy widow. I didn't have to remain in the delta; all that rich ranch land would bring a handsome price, and I'd be able to go anywhere, do anything.

Of course Joe would go with me. He'd want to, wouldn't he? Surely he would. And after all he'd done for me, I couldn't abandon him.

But Joe had ranching in his blood. It was all he knew, all he cared about. He'd spoken often enough of owning a place of his own, perhaps in the cattle country of eastern Montana. Was that what I wanted for myself, life with another rancher and in another hard and lonely place?

When I'd married Luke, all I wanted was love, a family to nurture, an untroubled life. Joe could offer me all of that. I'd told Annabelle Murdock that the delta was a harsh place that had bred a harsh man, but not everyone here was like Luke. His father had been a hard man who frequently beat him. Maybe it wasn't the delta but the lack of love that had turned him cruel and bitter and led him to take out his frustrations on me.

Seeing Joe lying there so helpless, having put his life on the line for me—not for the money, for me—I thought that perhaps I had enough love to make a new life with him no matter where it was. And it would be a good life, an untroubled life, with a good and gentle man.

I moved the rocker closer to the bed, slipped my hand under the quilt, and entwined my fingers with his rough, calloused ones. And soon dozed. . . .

"Missus Kraft?"

The man's voice seemed to come from far away. I moved my head from side to side against the rocker's high back, slowly opened my eyes. The first person I saw was Joe, still resting easily. Then, when I twisted around, I found myself looking at the peddler, James Shock.

"I didn't mean to startle you, sister," he said softly. His expression was grave, with no hint of the lustful gleam that had been in his bold stare earlier. "How is he?"

"He'll recover. Missus Devane saved his life."

"He'll have a doctor to look at him tomorrow. I'll see to that." He paused. "I'm sorry about your husband. But he left me no choice."

"I know that, Mister Shock."

He peered keenly at my face. "You look tired. How long have you been sitting here?"

I truly didn't know and I told him so.

"How would it be if I sat with him while you rest?"

I didn't want to leave Joe, but my body, bruised as it was, ached from sitting in the hard chair.

Perhaps I should lie down for a while. It seemed days since I'd last slept. "Thank you, Mister Shock. If you wouldn't mind."

"Not at all."

"You'll call me if he wakes? I'll be in the next room."

"Immediately, sister. Immediately."

I stood and, after brushing my hand across Joe's forehead—which was cool and dry now—I left the room.

The roadhouse was quiet, everyone in bed or asleep in the common room. Sometime while I'd dozed, the storm had slackened; the sound of the rain was a light pattering now. I opened the door to the second guest room. The lamp was still lit and I saw that Caroline Devane was still awake, sitting up on one of the two beds, crocheting an antimacassar of intricate design.

"Mister Hoover?" she asked.

"Still asleep. Mister Shock offered to sit with him so I can rest a bit."

"The accomodating Mister Shock."

"You don't care for him, do you?"

"Not very much, no."

"He saved our lives."

"It was his life he was interested in saving, not anyone else's."

"Perhaps. Does it really matter?" I lay down on the second bed and drew the counterpane over me. "Can't you sleep, Missus Devane?"

"No. As tired as I am, I have decisions to rethink. What has happened here tonight is sufficient to make one reconsider the wisdom of the course she's undertaken."

"I'm not sure I know what you mean."

She hesitated before speaking, the crochet needles clicking in the silence. Then, as if needing to unburden herself, she said: "Two years ago I had an affair with a friend of my husband. My marriage wasn't a brutal one like yours, it was simply . . . empty. I seldom saw John. He was in state government and constantly traveling from Sacramento to San Francisco. When he was at home, he ignored the children and me. I needed someone, and Hugh . . . well, he was everything John wasn't . . . kind, attentive, ardent. And so we became lovers. Our affair lasted six months."

"What happened then?"

"John found out about us."

"What did he do?"

"Immediately began divorce proceedings. The court awarded him custody of David and William, with virtually no visitation rights allowed me. Life in Sacramento soon became intolerable for me. You must be aware how society treats a divorcee, particularly one of an important man."

"Caroline, I'm so sorry. Did Hugh stand by you?"

"For a time. But he's a successful lawyer and the scandal was damaging to him, too. I no longer blame him for ending our relationship. He really had no choice."

"What will you do now?"

"The only member of my family who hasn't turned on me is my sister Mary. She and her husband have invited me to live with them on their farm in San Joaquin County. But I suspect they only want me as extra help with the chores and their seven children. It would be a hard life for me."

"Then why go there?" I said. "With your nurse's training . . ."

"That's what I've been considering. No one in Sacramento would allow me to practice. But this is a large country, and John's influence and the web of rumor only extend so far. If I could establish myself in a new city, rebuild my respectability, then perhaps once my children are old enough . . ." She sighed. "But it takes time and means to accomplish that. I have a great deal of the former, but none of the latter."

I was silent.

"Well, I've burdened you enough with my troubles," Caroline said. "You have far too many of your own, and you must be very tired. I'll let you sleep now. Perhaps I can, too."

But I didn't sleep right away. Joe was alive because of Caroline's ministrations; I owed her a debt of gratitude for that. I found myself thinking of the $3,000 I'd taken from Luke's safe. I no longer needed it now that Luke was dead and I was a wealthy widow. The money meant little to me, but it would mean a great deal to Caroline Devane. She was so desperately unhappy, just as I had been before Joe came into my life. My fortunes had changed, and it was in my power to change hers, too.

She wouldn't take the full amount if I tried to give it to her; she was too proud to accept money as a gift. But she might be persuaded if I offered part of it as a loan. I determined to speak to her about it in the morning, and not to take no for an answer.

T.J. MURDOCK

Traces of light began to seep in around the shutters on the bedroom window. Almost dawn. Sophie stirred beside me; I knew she'd also been awake for some time, even though she'd lain still and silent.

"Stopped raining," she said now.

"About an hour ago. Wind's died down, too."

"I heard you get up earlier."

"Checking on Joe Hoover. Missus Devane was there with him."

"How is he?"

"Alive and resting easy. No fever."

"She's a good nurse and a strong woman, troubled or not."

"Yes, but he still needs a doctor's attention. He

can't travel . . . we'll have to keep him here until the peddler can send Doc Kiley out from River Bend."

"That's right. Shock offered to return there this morning."

"Not for any selfless reasons, I suspect. He knows he has to report shooting Kraft to the sheriff, even with witnesses to back him up, before he can move on."

"Do you think the slough's passable yet?"

"Water seemed to be settling when I looked out earlier, but it's still running high and there's a lot of débris. I'll know better when it's light. We'll ferry the stage across as soon as it's safe."

She lay quietly again for a time. Then: "Nesbitt?"

"Too many people here now for him to do much except bide his time."

"If he doesn't speak to you right away, bring it out into the open yourself. We have to know what his intentions are."

"I will."

Blackbirds cried noisily somewhere outside—a sure sign that the weather had improved. When it was quiet again, Sophie said: "I'm not leaving you alone with him."

"You have to. If Nesbitt's bent on using that sidearm of his . . ."

"No. We'll put Annabelle on the stage in Pete's care, but I'm staying here. No matter what happens. I won't run again, Thomas, any more than you will."

I made no reply. I had told her about Boone Nesbitt last night, when we were alone in bed, and she'd said the same thing then—no more running and hiding, for either of us. There was no point in trying to argue with her when her mind was made up. Whatever happened with Nesbitt, we would face it together.

Eight years. Eight long, difficult years. We'd sought to convince ourselves that after so much time, this day might never come. And yet we'd never quite believed it. Patrick Bellright was a relentless, bitter, vengeful man with unlimited funds; he would never stop hunting me until his dying day. There would be a reward on my head, a large one, and it would carry no stipulations or caveats. Wanted—dead or alive.

It was a monstrous miscarriage of justice, the result of an accident that was not my fault, that I could not have avoided. A Sunday afternoon drive through Jackson Park in a rented carriage, a small child chasing a ball out of a line of shrubs and yelling loudly enough to frighten the horse. Thrashing hoofs, a scream, a crushed form sprawled in the roadway. We had rushed the child to the nearest doctor, even though Sophie and I were sure there was no life left in her. Marissa Bellright. Seven years old, and Patrick Bellright's only child.

The rest was nightmare. Dire threats, a murderous assault by one of his hirelings that I'd barely escaped. And then flight, again by bare escape, and arduous travel across country to this isolated backwater and a new, hardscrabble life as ferrymaster and innkeeper—labors as far removed from my former position as newspaper reporter and columnist as Chicago was from Twelve-Mile Crossing.

I had been a fool to submit my sketches for publication in San Francisco. Yet of all the possible ways I might be found by Bellright's hirelings, my pseudonymous writings had seemed the most remote. There was no way I could have anticipated a man like Nesbitt, whoever he was, making the connection between Harold P. Baxter and T.J. Murdock. But it had happened, and now it was too late. For me, but not, I vowed, for Annabelle or Sophie.

The dawn light was brightening. Sophie and I both rose, washed up, and dressed. She went to the kitchen to make coffee and get breakfast started, and I went to check on Hoover again. Mrs. Devane and Rachel Kraft were both with him now; the two women seemed to have developed a comradeship. There was no change in Hoover's condition.

Nesbitt was alone in the common room, stoking up the fire as he must have done throughout the night because the room was still warm. There was no sign of the peddler, Shock. As I crossed to the front door, Nesbitt stood up.

"We need to have a talk, Murdock," he said.

"Yes, but not right this second. I have work to attend to."

"Soon, though."

"I'll be around," I said. "I'm not going anywhere."

"I didn't suppose you were."

Outside, the yard was rain-puddled and littered with leaves and branches. The levee roads on both sides of the slough seemed to have survived intact, so far as I could see, although down toward where the slough bent to the south, the water level was only a couple of feet below the surface of the Middle Island road. Both embankments appeared to have held without crumbling. The slough waters were chocolate brown, frothy, still running fast and bobbing with tree limbs and other detritus from the storm.

I slogged through the mud to the landing. The barge was as I'd left it, moored fast, and the strung cable and windlass had come through undamaged. As I finished my examination, Pete Dell appeared from the direction of the barn. I went to meet him.

"How's she look out there, Murdock?"

"It should be safe enough for the stage to cross in another couple of hours."

"Good enough. I'm so far behind schedule now, couple more hours won't make any difference. Some wild night, eh?"

"In more ways than one."

"That peddler, Shock, is over in the barn hitching up his wagon."

"Already? He must be eager for an early start to River Bend."

"So he says. I don't much like that fella, tell you the truth."

"I would have said the same before he put an end to Luke Kraft's terrorism last night."

"Even so. But then, I never much liked Kraft, neither. His death's likely to cause a stir up Isleton way, even if he did deserve what he got." Pete stretched and blew on his hands. "Coffee ready?"

"Should be. Breakfast, too, just about."

We went on into the house. Two hours, I was thinking bleakly, and part of another for the stage to cross. And then Nesbitt. And then, one way or another, an end to my freedom.

JAMES SHOCK

I finished harnessing Nell to my wagon, hauled the Murdocks' buckboard to one side of the runway, opened the doors, and led Nell out of the barn. Bitter cold this morning, but I scarcely felt the bite. The $3,000, nestled inside my coat, provided warmth aplenty.

As I drove across the muddy yard, the ferrymaster stepped out of the roadhouse and hailed me. I drew to a stop, arranging my face in an expression of gravity. "I was about to stop in," I lied, "to ask after Mister Hoover."

"He's awake and taking nourishment. He passed a comfortable night."

"Well, he'll soon enough have the attention of a doctor."

"Good of you to make the trip to River Bend, Mister Shock."

"Not at all. I know my duty."

"Will you have breakfast before you go? Or at least a cup of hot coffee?"

"Thank you, no. I've no real appetite this morning, and I'd just as lief make tracks while the weather is dry. How much do I owe for the night's lodging?"

"Not a cent, under the circumstances."

"Christian of you, brother, but I insist on paying for your hospitality."

"As you please. Two dollars, then."

I leaned down to pay him. He thanked me and wished me Godspeed, and I touched my hat and gigged Nell up the muddy embankment. The wagon's wheels slipped a bit, but the old plug held her footing and soon enough we were on the levee road, headed in the direction of River Bend. I cast no backward glance.

Even if the money were missed, no one at the ferry crossing could be sure that I'd taken it; not even Nesbitt, if he was a lawman, would have cause or impetus to chase after me. I had only to pass through River Bend and I was safe. Sheriff, doctor? Hah! I wouldn't tarry in the town long enough to wave at a passer-by. Straight on through and back to Sacramento as quickly as I could get there.

I felt a song welling up in me and began to hum and then to sing softly. Later, when the day warmed a bit, I would bring out my banjo to celebrate properly my good fortune. Three thousand dollars, more than I'd ever had at one time. What a man could do with that much money! Why, I might just board Nell in a livery, put the wagon in storage, and take passage on one of the river packets to San Francisco. Yes, that was just what I'd do. A room in the city's best hotel, fine food, champagne, a pretty lass for company and bed. Heigh-ho! Life's bounties in abundance.

After a mile or so I passed a weed-infested side road that meandered off onto a long peninsula. Ahead was a sharp bend, both sides of the levee road shaded by sycamores. The road's surface was less slick here and we were clomping along at a right pert pace when we reached the bend and started through.

I didn't spy the downed tree until we were almost upon it. It lay blocking the road from one side to the other, its root-torn bole jutting high and its upper branches drooping down into the slough. I yanked back hard on the reins. Nell shied and the wagon slewed sideways, and, when that happened, just before we slid to a halt a few feet from the sycamore, something shifted and clattered inside. I could scarcely believe what I heard then—the startled, pained cry of a woman.

I set the brake, jumped down, ran to the rear of the wagon, and pulled open the doors. And lo, there she was, asprawl on the floor among a small litter of items dislodged from their hooks and cubbies, the hem of her traveling dress twisted up to reveal her drawers.

Annabelle Murdock.

"What the devil are you doing in my wagon?"

"Please don't be mad at me, James Never Jim Shock. Please!"

"Answer me, girl."

"I had to get away. I couldn't stay any longer. You'll let me come with you, won't you? I'll do anything you say. . . ."

"How did you get in there? The doors were locked."

"No, they weren't. I slipped out of the house and into the barn while it was still dark and the doors weren't locked, and I found a place to hide. . . ."

Damnation! I must have neglected to lock them when I brought out my banjo last night. Fury rose, hot and thick, in my chest and throat. Everything proceeding so well, and then the downed tree across the road and now this stupid priss of a girl. I wheeled away and stomped ahead to look at the sycamore. Blocking the road for fair, and a thick-trunked bugger it was. It would take a crew of men with axes and saws to cut it up and clear away the débris. The fury rose higher; my head commenced to throb with it, my hands to palsy some.

Annabelle had come out of the wagon and was standing, small and fearful, next to Nell. And fearful she should be, the little bitch. As if the blocked road wasn't enough of a trial, now I had this rattlebrain to contend with.

"You won't send me back?" she said. "Please say you won't send me back."

Send her back? Hell, no, I wouldn't. It was only a mile or so to the roadhouse, a short and easy walk, but once she arrived, there was no telling what she might say or the Murdocks might think. She may already have been missed. They might believe I'd enticed her away or, worse, kidnapped her. It was a risk I couldn't afford to take.

"James Never Jim Shock? Say you . . ."

"Don't call me that, you little bitch. Shut your damn' mouth and let me think."

A stifled gasp, and she was still.

Take her with me? I couldn't do that, either, even if the road were free for passage. She was a tender morsel, right enough, but under the age of legal consent. If I were caught with her, it would mean prison.

Turn the wagon around, drive it back to the crossing, take the ferry to Middle Island and points south? That was the logical choice, except for the $3,000. The money might already have been discovered missing, or the discovery made before I could make the crossing. Murdock, Dell, Nesbitt—a damned lawman, I was sure of it—and all of them armed. No, returning to the roadhouse was a fool's choice.

Nell. Unhitch her, ride her bareback over the obstruction, and into River Bend where I could secure better transportation. But she was old, slow, and anything but sure-footed, and the sycamore would have to be jumped rather than stepped across. And abandoning the wagon with all my wares and possessions was a galling prospect.

In my mouth was a foul taste, as if I'd been force-fed a plate of cowshit soup. What the bloody hell was I going to do?

"Mister Shock?" Timid now. I'd almost forgotten she was there.

"Didn't I tell you to keep your lip buttoned?"

"Are you going to send me back?"

No, I thought, *I'm going to put a bullet in your silly head and dump your body in the slough. Be rid of one problem, at the least.* I'd never killed a woman before, but there's a first time for everything, and she was a burden I couldn't bear. I eased back the tail of my coat.

"If you take me with you," she said, "I'll tell you how we can go on."

"Go on? With this blasted tree blocking the road?"

"There's a way around, another road that intersects with this one about a mile farther south."

"What road? You mean the one we passed a ways back?"

"Yes. It leads out to Crucifixion River."

"What's that?"

"It's . . . a kind of ghost camp."

"Nobody lives there?"

"Nobody."

"And the side road continues through it and back to the south of here?"

"No. There's another road in the camp, a track the people who lived there used."

"Easy to spot, this track?"

"It's overgrown. But I know where it is . . . I can show you."

"You're not lying to me?"

"No! I swear it."

I stared at her, long and hard. Her blue eyes were guileless. Some of my rage began to ease and I let the coattail fall closed. Her death sentence had been reprieved—for however long it took us to reach Crucifixion River.

CAROLINE DEVANE

Rachel was standing at Mr. Hoover's bedside when I went in to check on him. From her expression it was plain that she was upset and trying to hide it, but the reason was not her lover's condition. He was conscious, although not fully alert, and his color was good and his eyes clear. And his pulse, when I checked it, was strong.

The dressing on his wound needed changing. I removed the old one and was relieved to find no sign of infection. He would be all right until the doctor came from River Bend, and eventually, I thought, he would mend good as new. I put on more sulphur powder and a fresh bandage. His grimace prompted me to ask if he was in pain.

"Some," he said weakly, "but it's tolerable."

I gave him a spoonful of laudanum anyway, to help him sleep. He needed to rebuild his strength, and rest was the best remedy.

When I was done, Rachel squeezed his hand and whispered something to him that I deliberately did not listen to. Then she plucked at my sleeve and gestured toward the door. Whatever was upsetting her, she didn't wish to discuss it in front of Hoover. As soon as we were in the hallway, with the door closed, she said: "It's gone, Caroline."

"What is?"

"The money. The three thousand dollars I took

from my husband's safe. Joe had it in his belt pouch and now the pouch is empty."

I vaguely remembered seeing the pouch when Mr. Murdock and I had taken off Joe Hoover's jacket and shirt, but in my urgent need to extract the bullet and clean and dress the wound, I'd thought no more about it. "When did you learn this?"

"A few minutes ago, just before he woke up."

"Perhaps the Murdocks removed it for safekeeping."

"I don't think so. They'd have said something to me."

Yes, they would have. In the chaotic aftermath of Luke Kraft's sudden intrusion, I had forgotten his mention of the $3,000 and I suspected the Murdocks and the others had as well. All except one . . . and there was only one person among us that could be.

Rachel realized it at the same time. "James Shock," she said. "He took it last night."

Of course. Shock had slipped into the room, late, and talked her into leaving him there alone. Out of the goodness of his heart? Hardly. He was a cold-blooded opportunist, perfectly capable of taking note of the rancher's words and Hoover's belt pouch, and conniving to steal the money.

"Yes," I said, "but it's too late to confront him. Mister Murdock told me he drove off early to summon the doctor from River Bend."

"The money's gone for good, then. He won't stop in River Bend."

"Mister Murdock and Mister Nesbitt might be able to catch him on horseback. . . ."

"Why should they bother? It's not their place."

Footsteps, coming quickly from the family's quarters. Sophie Murdock appeared, her mouth set in grim lines.

"Have either of you seen my daughter?"

"Not at all this morning," I said, and Rachel shook her head. "She's not in her room?"

"No, and some of her things are missing. Clothing and her carpetbag."

"Oh, Lord. You think she may have run off?"

"I don't know. It's possible. She's young and restless, she dislikes her life here, and after what happened last night . . ."

I recalled the adoring looks Annabelle had lavished on James Shock. Was it possible that he'd sweet-talked her into leaving with him? Or that she'd decided to join him on her own?

My face must have betrayed what I was thinking. "What is it, Missus Devane?" Sophie Murdock asked. "Do you have an idea where Annabelle's gone?"

"Yes," I said, "I'm afraid I do."

BOONE NESBITT

I was out in the livery barn, watching Murdock help Pete Dell harness the stage team, when Mrs. Murdock came rushing in. The look of her was both frantic and frightened. "Thomas," she said to her husband, "Annabelle's gone."

"What do you mean . . . gone?"

"She's nowhere on the property, and some of her clothes and her carpetbag are missing. But that's not all. Missus Kraft just told me Joe Hoover was carrying three thousand dollars in a belt pouch, the money her husband was shouting about last night, and that's missing, too."

"My God, you don't believe Annabelle stole it?"

"I don't know what to believe."

"She'd never do such a thing. She's not a thief."

Mrs. Murdock was looking at the stalls. "The saddle horses . . . they're all here."

"Yes, and she's not foolish enough to go traipsing off on foot."

"Missus Devane thinks she may be with the peddler, Shock."

"What!"

"Missus Devane may be right," I said. "Shock was in a hurry to pull out this morning. Stolen money in his pocket and maybe the girl hidden in his wagon could be the real reason."

"What're you saying, Nesbitt? That he kidnapped my daughter?"

"More likely she went of her own free will, with or without his knowledge."

Murdock said grimly: "Well, I'll find out. It's been less than two hours since Shock drove out and he can't make fast time in that wagon of his. With luck I can catch him on horseback before he reaches River Bend."

"I'll go with you," I said. "Shock's fast with that revolver of his, and a crack shot. Two makes better odds."

"Three makes better still," Pete Dell said.

"Murdock and I can do the job. Best if you stay here with the women."

"You hand out orders real easy, mister. Who put you in charge?"

"Don't argue with him, Pete," Murdock said. "We don't have any time to waste."

He sent his wife into the house for his sidearm and shell belt; I was already wearing mine. I saddled the rented piebald. Murdock didn't own a decent saddle horse, but Luke Kraft's roan gelding was broke enough to let a stranger throw Kraft's old McClellan saddle on his back and climb aboard. We were out of the barn and on the levee road inside of five minutes.

The road was in reasonably good shape after the storm. Rain-puddled and muddy, so we couldn't run the animals even though it chafed Murdock not to. I set the pace at a steady lope that was still some faster than Shock could drive that peddler's wagon of his, and we had no trouble maintaining it.

Mostly we rode in silence, except for one brief exchange. Murdock twisted his head my way and said: "Just who are you, Nesbitt?"

"Does it matter?"

"You talk and act like a lawman. Are you one?"

"In a way. I work for the Pinkertons."

"So that's it. That's how you knew about me."

"We'll talk about that later."

"Does Bellright know yet?"

"Not yet."

"All for yourself, eh? How much are you getting for me, dead or alive? Five thousand? Ten? More?"

"Later, Murdock. Keep your mind on Shock and your daughter for now."

The morning was cold and gray, the débris-choked slough waters on both sides receding and mist rising here and there from the half-drowned cat-tails along the banks. Birds screeched and chattered, frogs croaked long and loud—the only sounds that reached my ears. We had the road to ourselves, but there were fresh wheel and hoof tracks to mark the passage of Shock's wagon.

I slowed as we passed a side road that cut away through a swampy peninsula to the north. There were no tracks at the entrance to the road, but the grass and pig weed farther on seemed to be mashed down in places. I kept us riding ahead because I couldn't think of a reason for Shock to have detoured onto a side road—not until we rounded a bend and came on the fallen sycamore.

"That tree's been down a while," Murdock said. "There's no way Shock could have gotten his wagon around it."

"He didn't," I said. "He doubled back to that side road we passed. Where does it lead?"

"Crucifixion River. What's left of it."

"Any other way out of there?"

"An overgrown track the sect members used. But Shock wouldn't know about that."

"Your daughter does, though, doesn't she?"

"Yes," he said, tight-lipped. "Annabelle knows."

We rode back to the intersection. As we turned onto the Crucifixion River road, I leaned down for a better look at the ground. Up close you could see where Shock had tried to rub out and hide the wagon tracks at the turning. A short ways beyond I spied a pile of horse manure that still steamed in the cold air. We couldn't be far behind them now, I judged.

I said as much to Murdock, and, riding as fast as we dared, we followed the wagon tracks through the wet grass and swampy earth.

ANNABELLE MURDOCK

I sat forward as Crucifixion River came into view ahead. It was an awful, bleak place in the best of weather, and on a dark gray day like this one the look of it made me shiver and hunch up even more inside my black dog coat. Except for marsh birds, the quiet was eerie. You could almost hear the people singing "We Shall Gather at the River," the way they had been the day they arrived and Dad and Mother ferried them across the slough. I was just a little girl then, but I still remembered the singing and it still gave me chills.

There was a big weedy meadow where the road ended, stretching out along the banks of the mud-brown river. At one end were the remnants of the potato and corn and vegetable patches the sect people had started, and at the other was a church or meeting house and about a dozen cabins built back among willows and swamp oaks. There wasn't much left of the buildings now. After the people moved away, shanty boaters had come in and carted off everything that was left behind. Even doors, window coverings, floorboards. They were all just hollow shells now, some of them with collapsed walls and roofs. Dead things waiting for the swampland and the river to swallow them up.

"Now isn't this a pretty spot," James Shock said.

Pretty? It was like visiting a cemetery.

But I didn't say anything. I hadn't looked at him since we left the levee road and I didn't look at him now. I sat away over on the wagon seat, as far away from him as I could get, and hunched and hugged myself and tried not to think what was going to happen.

He wasn't James Never Jim Shock to me any more. He wasn't a handsome, romantic, banjo-playing traveling man; he was just a peddler and a cold-souled, foul-mouthed killer, and I didn't know how I ever could have believed he was a man to run away with and give my favors to. Shame made my face and neck flush hot. I *wasn't* ready to leave the delta yet, on my own or with anybody. I knew that now. What an addle-pated fool I'd been!

I kept remembering the way he'd talked and the look on his face when he found me in the wagon, as if I were a bratty child instead of a woman—as if he'd like nothing better than to paddle my backside, or do something even worse to me. His eyes—Lord, that cold, ugly stare! It wasn't anything at all like the way his eyes had been in the common room last night. That James Shock had been a sham, a sweet-talking wolf in sheep's clothing. This was the real James Shock, sitting next to me right now. And I was as purely scared of him as I'd been of anything in my whole life.

"This road just ended," he said. "And I don't see any other."

I gestured without looking at him. "It runs through that motte of swamp oak down along the river, on the far side of the meeting house."

"It better had. And it better lead where you say, back to the levee road."

"Why would I lie to you?"

"Well, that's right, now, isn't it? You wouldn't have any reason to lie."

"None at all. What . . . what are you going to do with me?"

He didn't answer, just snapped the reins and clattered us across the meadow toward the meeting house. We were almost there, angling past the big empty shell, when he shifted around in a way that made me cast a quick glance in his direction. He was holding the reins in his left hand and he'd moved his right down and was pulling the tail of his coat back, reaching inside to his belt.

I don't know how I knew he was about to draw his revolver, and what he intended to do with it, but I did know, all at once, and never mind that I couldn't see any rhyme or reason for him to want to harm me. I just knew, with a certainty that made the hair on my scalp stand straight up, that he was planning to kill me as soon as he was sure of where that other road was.

I'd been scared before. Now I was terrified.

"Annabelle? You sure, now, the road starts in that motte of trees?"

I couldn't have spoken if I'd tried. And I didn't

dare sit there next to him a second longer. My only hope was to jump off the wagon and try to get away from him, and that was what I did, quick as a cat.

I landed all right on both feet, but then I lost my balance and sprawled headlong in the wet grass. Shock yelled something, but I didn't listen to it. I rolled over and pulled my legs under me and lifted my skirts and ran as fast as I'd ever run, away from the wagon toward the meeting house.

The open doorway yawned ahead. I was almost there, almost safe. . . .

And then—oh, God!—he started shooting at me.

T.J. MURDOCK

The first two shots sounded, faint and echoing in the morning stillness, when we were a few hundred rods from the camp. I pulled back hard on the reins; so did Nesbitt. The ghost buildings weren't within sight yet, hidden behind a screen of trees ahead.

"Small caliber," he said. "Handgun, not a rifle."

"Christ!"

"Can't be Shock. What would he be firing at?"

"Nobody else out here."

"Hunters, shanty boaters?"

"Not this soon after a big storm."

Another shot cracked.

My heart slammed and my mouth turned dry as dust. I kicked Kraft's roan into a run, no longer mindful of the boggy ground. Nesbitt was right behind me. I had stopped caring what happened to me, but Annabelle . . . if anything happened to Annabelle . . .

JAMES SHOCK

The little bitch had caught me by surprise, jumping off the wagon that way. I yanked Nell to a halt, dragged on the brake with my left hand, and drew the revolver with my right. I had it out quickly enough, while she was still running, but haste threw off my aim. The round missed wide, tearing splinters from the building wall. I steadied my arm and fired again just as she ducked through the doorway inside. I couldn't tell if I'd hit her or not.

Cursing, I hauled the Greener out from under the seat and jumped down and ran over to the tumble-down building. By grab, I'd blow her damned head off when I caught her.

ANNABELLE MURDOCK

Hide!

But there was nowhere to hide in the meeting house. It was just one big room, with no partitions or cubbyholes and a section of the roof gone and a hole in the back wall where the fireplace had collapsed.

I couldn't stay here. I had to get out quick and find some place else. The woods, one of the other cabins, any place where Shock wouldn't find me. I wasn't hurt, but I'd felt the heat of the second bullet on my cheek as it whizzed by. I was so scared I thought I might wet myself.

Enough daylight came in through the holes so that I could see well enough. There wasn't anything on the uneven floor but weeds and animal droppings and pools of rain water. I stumbled across it to the jumble of fireplace stones, clambered and clawed my way over and through them to the opening in the wall. My foot slipped before I reached it and my knee knocked hard on one of the rocks.

And just as that happened, I heard a *thwack* above my head and then the bark of Shock's revolver behind me.

Gasping, sobbing, I crawled over the rest of the stones and flung myself through the hole, tearing a long rip in the sleeve of my coat. My knee burned like fire, but I didn't care as I scrambled to my feet. All I could think was—run!

Run, run, run!

BOONE NESBITT

Kraft's roan was a better horse than the piebald and Murdock was ten rods ahead when we cleared the trees and Crucifixion River came into view. But I had only a peripheral look at the crumbling ghost camp and Shock's wagon stopped in the open meadow. What caught and held my attention was the girl staggering across open ground between the shell of a large building and a cluster of decaying shacks squatting among the trees.

"Annabelle!"

It was Murdock who yelled her name. We both veered sharply in her direction, guns already filling our hands. She heard us coming, twisted her head in our direction, but she had the sense not to slow up any. Shock was chasing her; in the next second, he came busting through a hole in the sagging back wall of the large building, brandishing a shotgun.

He spied us before he'd taken half a dozen steps. He swung around, crouching, as Murdock bore down on him. I pulled up hard just as Murdock fired—a wild shot, like most from the back of a running horse. Shock didn't even flinch. He let go with one barrel of the Greener, and the spray of buckshot knocked Murdock off the roan's back and sent him rolling through the grass.

I swung out of leather. If the ground hadn't been

wet and slick, I would've been able to set myself for a quick, clear shot at Shock. As it was, my boots slid out from under me and I went down hard enough on my backside to jar the Colt loose from my grip. It landed a few feet away, and by the time I located it and started to scrabble toward it, Shock was up and moving my way with that Greener leveled.

I heard him say—"All right, you son-of-a-bitch."—as I got my hand on the Colt, and I was cold sure it was too late, I was a dead man.

Only it didn't happen that way.

It was Shock who died in that next second.

Murdock was hurt, but the buckshot hadn't done him enough damage to keep him out of the play. He'd struggled up onto one knee and he put a slug clean through Shock's head at thirty paces. The Greener's second barrel emptied with a roar, but the buckshot went straight down as he was falling. Dead and on his way to hell before he hit the ground.

I got up slowly, went over to him for a quick look to make sure, then holstered my weapon, and went to Murdock's side. He squinted up me, his jaw clenched tightly. There was blood and buckshot holes on his left arm and shoulder and the side of his neck, but he wasn't torn up as badly as he might've been.

"Dad! Dad!"

Annabelle. She'd seen it happen, and, now that

it was finished, she'd come running. She dropped down beside him, weeping, and he hugged her and crooned a little the way a relieved father does when he sees his child is unharmed.

There were some things I wanted to say to Murdock, but this wasn't the time or place. I turned away from them and went to where the peddler's wagon stood in the meadow, to see what I could find to treat Murdock's wounds.

ANNABELLE MURDOCK

I huddled in my bed, the quilt drawn tightly around me. My scrapes and bruises hurt, but not nearly as much as my conscience. For a while after we got back from Crucifixion River in the peddler's wagon, I'd cried and felt sorry for myself, but I wasn't feeling sorry for *me* any more. . . .

A tap on the door and Mother came in. I asked her how Dad was, and she said she and Mrs. Devane had gotten all the buckshot out of his arm and shoulder and she'd given him some laudanum for the pain.

"He's going to be all right, isn't he?"

"Of course he is. He and Mister Hoover both."

I said: "It's all my fault." And then—fool that I am—I started crying again. "If I hadn't fallen for James Shock and hidden in his wagon, Dad wouldn't've been shot. I did an awful thing, and he could have died and so could I."

Mother sat beside me and patted my back, just as she'd done when I was a little girl and had hurt myself. It only made me sob harder. I felt like a child right now. A *bad* one.

She said: "That's true enough. But we've made you live such a sheltered, isolated life, you couldn't possibly know what a wicked man that peddler was. And you've never made a secret of how much you want to leave the delta."

"Maybe it's not so bad here, after all." But I didn't really believe that. Did Mother? I didn't think so, but she'd made the best of the past eight years in this place. So had Dad. The least I could do was the same while I was still living here.

I wasn't crying any more. I wiped my eyes with a corner of the sheet and said: "Someday I may still want to go to San Francisco, have a different kind of life. You'd understand, wouldn't you?"

"Of course we would. But you'll tell us when the time comes, let us help you? You won't try to run away again?"

"No, Mother, I've learned my lesson," I said, and I meant it. "I'll never run away again, not ever."

RACHEL KRAFT

I walked out of the roadhouse as the driver was bringing the stage around from the livery barn. Caroline Devane, wearing a gray serge traveling dress, stood still as a statue looking out over Twelve-Mile Slough, her crocheting bag and reticule beside her; the wind blew wisps of her hair, and her gaze was remote, as if she'd already traveled many miles from here.

I said her name, and she turned and gave me a wan smile. "Have you made a decision about your future?"

"Yes. I'm going on to my sister and her family, because they're expecting me, but I won't stay long. There's a shortage of trained nurses in this state. I ought to be able to find employment in Los Angeles or San Diego."

"Do you have enough money to live until you do?"

"Enough, if I'm fortunate. Before I left Sacramento, I sold my jewelry."

Mr. Nesbitt had returned the $3,000 to me when he and Annabelle and poor Mr. Murdock came back with word of the peddler's death, and, after talking to Joe, I'd put the money into his belt pouch. Now I pressed the pouch into Caroline's hands.

"Perhaps this will help."

She stared down at it, then opened it. Her eyes widened with astonishment when she saw the bills and specie inside.

"It's half the money I took from my husband's safe," I said. "Fifteen hundred dollars."

"I can't accept it." She closed the pouch and thrust it back at me. "Why would you want to give me so much money?"

"You saved Joe's life."

"I only did what I was trained to do."

"Please take it. Joe and I want you to have it."

"No, I wouldn't feel right. . . ."

"Please."

Our eyes locked—two stubborn, proud women.

"You're going away," she said, "you'll need it. . . ."

"I'm not going away and I don't need it. Joe and I decided to return to the ranch when he's able to travel. My late husband's affairs have to be put in order and there are other things that need attending to. After that . . . well, we'll see."

"Still, I can't take money from you. . . ."

"It's not a gift, it's a loan. I can have a paper drawn up to that effect if you like."

"But you hardly know me. . . ."

"I know enough. You're good and honest and caring and you've already paid a high price for your sins. You shouldn't have to pay any more."

"I . . . I don't know what to say. . . ."

"Say yes. It will make starting your new life so much easier."

She was silent for several seconds. Then, slowly: "Well, if it's to be a loan . . ."

"From one new friend to another."

I pressed the pouch into her hands again. This time she kept it, her eyes bright with tears.

Two stubborn, proud women, one strong, the other learning how to be.

T.J. MURDOCK

In the darkened bedroom I lay waiting for the pain in my bandaged shoulder to ease. It had been a long, rough ride in Shock's wagon with Nesbitt driving and Annabelle making me as comfortable as she could inside, and the removal of the buckshot and treatment of my wounds had been another ordeal. But all I cared about, then and now, was that Annabelle was safe and unhurt.

"How're you feeling, Murdock?"

Nesbitt. I hadn't even heard him come in. If I'd been more alert, I might have been surprised to see that he wore one of my old, grease-stained dusters, unbuttoned, over a black broadcloth suit.

"Drowsy," I said. "Sophie gave me laudanum."

"You'll have a doctor soon enough. You and Hoover both."

"I won't be in any shape to travel for a few days. You figure on staying here until then?"

Instead of answering, he said: "Pete Dell's ready to travel right now. I told your wife I'd help her and Annabelle winch the stage across to Middle Island."

"That why you're wearing my duster?"

"That's why." There was a little silence and I could feel the pain dulling, my eyelids growing heavy. Then he said: "I owe you thanks for saving my life in Crucifixion River. Another second and Shock would've blown my head off with that Greener."

"I know it."

"You could've waited and let that happen before you shot him. Some men in your position would have, to save their own hides."

"I'm not one of them."

"No," he said, "you're not. Not the kind of man Patrick Bellright thinks you are at all."

"Won't make any difference to him when you hand me over."

"I won't be handing you over."

I wasn't sure I'd heard him right. "Say that again."

"I'm not giving you to Bellright," Nesbitt said. "Seems I made a mistake . . . you're not Harold P. Baxter, you're T.J. Murdock. Soon as the stage is ferried across, I'll be heading to River Bend to talk to the sheriff and send you a doctor, then on back to San Francisco."

"But . . . the reward . . . ?"

112

"To hell with the reward. I've gotten along well enough on a Pinkerton salary and I'll keep right on getting along. I don't need a piece of land in the Valley of the Moon."

I was too numb to ask what that meant. All I could manage was: "Why?"

"You saved my life, now I'm returning the favor. Simple as that. And you can quit worrying about somebody else like me finding you. It's not likely to happen, and, even if it did, it'd have to be before next summer. After that it won't matter."

"Won't matter? What do you mean?"

"I checked up on Bellright before I came out here. The old bugger's dying of cancer. He'll be gone in six months and his vendetta with him." Nesbitt went to the door, then stopped again long enough to say: "I hope you keep on writing for the *Argonaut* and *The Overland Monthly*, Murdock. I really do enjoy those sketches of yours."

Then he went out and left me to the first real peace I'd known in eight long years.

FREE DURT

by Bill Pronzini

They were out for a Saturday drive on the county's back roads when they saw the sign. It was angled into the ground next to a rutted access lane that wound back into the hills—crudely made from a square of weathered plywood nailed to a post. The two words on it had been hand-drawn, none too neatly, with black paint.

FREE DURT

Ramage laughed out loud. "Look at that, will you? Proof positive of the dumbing-down of America."

"Oh, don't be so superior," Carolyn said. "Lots of people can't spell. That doesn't mean they're illiterate."

"D-u-r-t? A five-year-old kid can spell dirt correctly."

"Not everyone's had the benefits of a college education, you know. Or a cushy white-collar job."

"Cushy? Any time you want to trade, you let me know. I'd damn' well rather be a school administrator than an ad-agency copy writer any day."

"Sure. At half the salary."

"Beside the point, anyway," Ramage said. "We were talking about that sign. Whoever made it couldn't've got past the first grade . . . that's the point."

"You can be such a snob sometimes," she said. Then: "I wonder why they're giving it away?"

"Giving what away? You mean dirt?"

"Well, out here in the country like this. Why don't they just spread it over the fields or something?"

"That's a good question."

"And where did they get so much that they have to give it away for nothing? Some kind of construction project?"

"Could be." He slowed the BMW, began looking for a place to turn around. "Let's go find out."

"Oh, now, Sam . . ."

"Why not? I'd like to know the answer myself. And I'd like to meet somebody who doesn't know how to spell dirt."

She put up an argument, but he didn't pay any attention. He drove back to the rutted lane, turned into it. It meandered through a grassy meadow, up over the brow of a hill, and down the other side. From the crest they could see the farm below, nestled in a wide hollow flanked on one side by a willow-banked creek and on the other by a small orchard of some kind. The layout surprised Ramage. He'd expected a little place, run-down or close to it, something out of Appalachia West. He couldn't have been more wrong.

It wasn't just that the farm was large—farmhouse, big barn, smaller barn, chicken coop, two other outbuildings, a vegetable garden, the rows of fruit trees, fences around the house and along the lane farther down and marching across the nearby fields. It was that everything was pristine. The buildings, the fences gleamed with fresh coats of white paint. The wire in the chicken run looked new. There wasn't anything in sight that seemed old or worn or out of place.

"Whoever owns this may not know how to spell," Carolyn said, "but they certainly know how to keep things in apple-pie order."

Ramage drove down between the fences and into the farmyard. A dog began to bark somewhere in the house as he nosed the BMW up near the front gate. Once he shut off the engine, the noise of the dogs and the clucking of chickens and the murmur of an afternoon breeze were the only sounds.

They got out of the car. The front door of the house opened just then and a man came out with a dog on a chain leash. When Ramage got a good look at the man, he thought wryly: *Now that's more like it. Farmer from top to bottom, like the one in the Grant Wood painting. In his sixties, tall, stringy, with a prominent Adam's apple and a face like an old, seamed baseball glove. He's even wearing overalls.*

As he brought the dog out through the gate,

Carolyn moved close to Ramage and a little behind him. Big dogs made her twitchy. This one was pretty big, all right, some kind of Rottweiler mix, probably, but it didn't look very fierce. Just a shaggy farm dog, the only difference being that its coat was better groomed than most and it didn't make a sound now that it was leashed.

"Howdy, old-timer," Ramage said to the farmer. "How you doing?"

"Howdy yourself."

"We were driving by and saw your sign down by the road."

"Figured as much. Brings visitors up every now and then."

"I'll bet it does."

"Interested in free dirt, are you?"

"Might be."

"Can't get but a couple of sacks in that little car of yours."

"We couldn't use any more than that. You the owner here?"

"That's right. Name's Peete. Last name, three e's."

"Sam Ramage. This is my girlfriend, Carolyn White."

Carolyn gave him a look. She didn't like the word girlfriend. Ms. Feminist. But, hell, that was what she was, wasn't it?

"What's the dog's name?"

"Buck."

"He doesn't bite, does he?" Carolyn asked.

"Not unless I tell him to. Or unless you try to bite him."

That made her smile. "You have a nice place here, Mister Peete."

"Suits me."

"Must take a lot of work to keep everything so spick-and-span."

"Does. Always something that needs tending to."

"Keeps you and your hired hands busy, I'll bet."

"Don't have any hired hands," Peete said.

"Really? Just you and your family, then?"

"No family, neither."

"You mean you live here alone?"

"Me and Buck."

"Must be kind of a lonely life, 'way out here, if you don't mind my saying so."

"I like it. Don't like people much." Peete was looking at Ramage's right hand. "Some trick you got there, young fella," he said.

Ramage grinned. He'd been knuckle-rolling his lucky coin back and forth across the tops of his fingers, making it disappear into his palm and then reappear again on the other side.

"That's his only trick," Carolyn said. "He's so proud of it he has to show it off to everybody he meets."

"Don't pay any attention to her. Her only trick is running her mouth."

"Never seen a coin like that," Peete said. "What kind is it?"

"Spanish doubloon. I picked it up in the Caribbean a couple of years ago."

"Genuine?"

"Absolutely." Ramage did three more quick finger rolls, made the coin disappear into his hand, and then into his pocket. "I don't see this free dirt of yours, old-timer. Where have you got it?"

"Barn yonder."

"Let's have a look."

Peete led them across the farmyard to the smaller of the two gleaming white barns, the big dog trotting silently at his side.

On the way Ramage asked conversationally: "What do you keep in the big barn? Cows?"

"Don't have any cows."

"Sheep? Goats?"

"No livestock except chickens. Big barn's for storage."

"Farm equipment?"

"Among other things."

When they reached the smaller barn, Peete unlatched the double doors and swung one of the halves open. Ramage could smell the dirt before he saw it, a kind of heavy, loamy odor in the gloom. It was piled high between a pair of tall wood partitions, not as much as he'd expected, but a pretty large hunk of real estate just the same—ten feet long, maybe twenty wide, by seven or eight feet high. He moved closer. Mixture of clods and loose earth, all dark brown with reddish highlights. Some of it toward the bottom had a crusty look, as if it had been there for a while; the rest seemed more or less fresh.

"What makes this dirt so special?" he asked the farmer.

"Special?"

"Well, there's a lot of it, and you keep it in here instead of outside, and you give it away free. How come?"

"Best there is. Rich. Good for gardens, lawns."

"So why don't you use it yourself, on that vegetable garden behind the house?"

"I do. Got more than I need."

"Where does it come from?" Carolyn asked. "Some place on your property?"

"Yep. Truck it in from the cemetery."

She blinked. "From the . . . did you say cemetery?"

"That's right. It's graveyard dirt."

There was a little silence before Ramage said: "You're kidding."

"No, sir. Gospel truth."

"Graveyard dirt?"

"Yep."

"From a cemetery on your property?"

"Yep. Old Indian burial ground."

"Never heard of any Indian tribes around here."

"Long time ago. Miwoks."

Carolyn asked: "You don't desecrate the graves, do you? Just so you can carry off a lot of rich soil?"

"Nope. Do my digging in the cemetery, but not where the graves are."

"How can you be sure?"

"I'm sure. You would be, too, if you saw the place."

"Miwoks?" Ramage said. "I didn't think they ranged this far south."

"Nomadic bunch, must've been."

"Nomads don't build cemeteries for their dead."

Peete fixed him with a squinty look. "Don't believe there's a burial ground close by, that it?"

"Let's just say I'm skeptical."

"Prove it to you, if you want," Peete said. "Take you over and show it to you."

"Yeah? How far away is it?"

"Not far. Won't take long."

Ramage looked at Carolyn.

"Oh, no," she said, "count me out."

"Real interesting spot," Peete said. "Artifacts and things."

"What kind of artifacts?" Ramage asked.

"Arrowheads, bowls, pots. Just lying around."

"Uhn-huh."

"Fact. See for yourself."

"Not me," Carolyn said. "I don't like cemeteries. And I've seen all the Native American artifacts I care to see."

"No damn' spirit of adventure," Ramage said.

"You go ahead if you want. I'm staying right here."

She meant it. And when she got stubborn about something, you couldn't change her mind for love or money.

Ramage said disgustedly: "All right, the hell with it. I guess we'll have to take your word for it, old-timer. About the dirt and the burial ground, both."

"Some do, some don't. Suit yourself."

"For now, anyway," Ramage added. "Maybe some other time."

"Any time you want to see it." Peete gestured at the pile of free dirt. "How many sacks you want?"

"None right now. Some other time on that, too."

Peete shrugged, led them out of the barn into the sunshine. He closed the doors, set the latch, and started to move off.

"Hold on a second," Ramage said. And when the farmer stopped and glanced back at him: "About that sign of yours, down by the road."

"What about it?"

"Don't take offense, but you misspelled dirt."

"That a fact?"

"It's with an I, not a u. D-i-r-t. You might want to correct it."

"Then again," Peete said, "I might not."

He took the dog away to the house without a backward glance.

Carolyn said: "Did you have to bring up that sign?"

Ramage ignored her until they were in the car, bouncing down the rutted lane. Then he said, more to himself than to her: "Some character, that Peete."

"You think he's just a dumb hick, I suppose."

"Don't you?"

"No. I think he's a lot smarter than you give him credit for."

"Because of that business with the dirt and the Indian burial ground? I didn't believe it for a minute."

"Well, neither did I," she said. "That's the real reason I didn't want to go along with him. The whole thing's a hoax, a game he plays with gullible tourists. I wouldn't be surprised if he misspelled dirt on that sign just to draw people like us up here."

"Might have at that."

"If we'd gone along with him, what he'd've shown us is some spot he faked up with Native American artifacts and phony graves."

"Just to get a good laugh at our expense?"

"Some people have a warped sense of humor."

"Didn't look like Peete had any sense of humor."

"You can't tell what a person's like inside from the face they wear in public. You ought to know that."

"I'd still like to've seen the place," Ramage said.

"Why, for heaven's sake?"

"Satisfy my curiosity."

"You'd've been playing right into his hand."

"Still . . . I can't help being curious, can I?"

He stayed curious all that day, and the next, and the next after that. About the fake Miwok burial ground, and about Peete, too. How could the old buzzard afford to pay for all the upkeep on that farm of his, and give away good rich soil, when he had no help and no livestock except for a few chickens? Crops like alfalfa, fruit from that small orchard? Maybe he ought to drive back out there, alone this time, and have a look at the "cemetery" and see what else he could find out.

On Friday afternoon, Ramage decided that that was just what he was going to do.

The snotty young fella named Coolidge said: "I don't believe it."

"Gospel truth."

"Graveyard dirt from some old Indian cemetery?"

"Every inch of it."

"And you truck it in here and hoard it so you can give it away free. You think I was born yesterday, pop?"

"Prove it to you, if you want."

"How you going to do that?"

"Burial ground's not far from here," Peete said. "Other side of that hill yonder."

"And you want me to go see it with you."

"Up to you. Only take a few minutes."

Coolidge thought about it. Then he grinned crookedly and said: "All right, for free d-u-r-t, why not? What have I got to lose?"

"That's right," Peete said. He tightened his grip on Buck's chain, tossed his new lucky piece into the air with his other hand. Sunlight struck golden glints from the doubloon before he caught it with a quick downward swipe. "What have you got to lose?"

HE SAID . . . SHE SAID

by Marcia Muller

Cal Hartley heaved the last of the five-gallon water jugs into the back of his van and slammed the rear doors. Then he coiled the hose onto its holder on the spigot. As he got into the driver's seat, he glanced across the parking lot at the White Iron Chamber of Commerce building; only two cars were there, both belonging to employees, and no one had seen him filling up, or else they'd have come outside by now, wanting to know where their so-called voluntary donation was. Three bucks well saved.

At the stop sign at the main highway, Cal hesitated. East toward home? West toward town, where he'd earlier run some errands? West. He didn't feel like going home yet. Home was not where the heart was these days.

The Walleye Tavern was dark and cool on this bright, hot August afternoon. Abel Arneson, the owner and sole occupant, stood behind the bar under one of the large stuffed pike that adorned the pine walls, staring up at a Twins game on the TV mounted at the room's far end. When he saw Cal enter, he reached for a remote and turned the sound down.

"What brings you to town, Professor?" he asked. "Professor" because Cal was a former faculty member of the University of Minnesota, recently moved north from Minneapolis to the outskirts of this small town near the Boundary Waters National Canoe Area.

"Water run. Hardware store. Calls on the cell phone. It doesn't work outside of town." Cal slid onto a stool. In spite of him and Abel being native Minnesotans, their patterns of speech could not have been more different. Cal sounded pure, flat middle America, while Abel spoke with the rounded, vaguely Scandinavian accent of the Iron Range.

Abel, a big man with thinning white hair and thick horn-rimmed glasses, set a bottle of Leinenkugel in front of Cal. "Not so easy, living without running water, huh?"

"Not so bad. The lake makes a good bathtub, and we've got a chemical toilet. All we need the fresh water for is brushing our teeth, cooking, washing dishes."

"And from the hardware store?"

Cal smiled wryly. "Heavy-duty extension cords. I think I told you the power company allowed us to hook into the pole up on the road till we finish with our renovations. Seems like we need more cords every day."

Abel shook his head, looked at his watch, and poured himself a shot of vodka. "I don't envy you, trying to bring back that old, run-down lodge. Thirty-five years abandoned by old lady Mott, just sitting there rotting. Some folks around here say it's cursed."

"Yeah, I've heard that. But I don't believe in curses."

"No?"

"Definitely not. A place is only what you make it. You saw the main building when you came out. It's livable and will be a fine home eventually. We think we can save three of the cabins for when our kids and . . . someday . . . grandkids come to visit. The rest we're demolishing."

"By yourselves? Didn't any of those contractors I referred you to get back with estimates?"

"The roofer, and he's done already. The others we only need for the septic system, plumbing, and electrical. They'll be in touch."

"Your wife . . . Maggie, is it?"

"Right."

"She doesn't seem the type for hard labor. Wasn't she some kind of artist in the Twin Cities?"

"Interior designer."

"How does she feel being dragged off to the end of the road here?"

Cal felt his throat tighten up. He took a sip of beer before he said: "She feels just fine. It was her idea, in fact. She found the property."

"Good for her." Abel looked up at the TV, reached for the remote, and turned the volume up slightly.

Good for her. Yeah, right. You won't say that when I tell you she's trying to kill me.

Maggie was painting the floor of the one-room cabin with red enamel when Howie, her black Lab, ran in and stepped on the wet surface.

"Howie!" she yelled, and the dog—perverse creature—began to wag his tail and knocked over the paint can. Maggie stood up, shooed him out the door, and wiped her damp brow with the back of her hand. It must have been ninety-five degrees, and the humidity was trying to match the temperature.

She regarded the mess on the floor, then turned away and went outside. The red paint had seemed a good idea two days ago—it would conceal the poor quality of the wood and the indelible stains from years of a leaking roof, plus lend a cheerful note to a cabin that was perpetually dark because of the overhanging white pines—but now she decided she didn't really like it. Better brown, or even gray, covered in colorful rag rugs from the White Iron Trading Post.

She stood in the shade of the trees and looked down the gradual slope to what had once been the main building of Sunrise Lodge. A long two-story log structure with many-paned windows and a sagging porch, it sat in a clearing halfway between this cabin and the shore of Lost Wolf Lake. Over the thirty-five years that the property had sat abandoned, pines and scrub vegetation had grown up, so only a sliver of blue water was visible from the porch's once-excellent vantage point. In time, the trees would be cleared, but first the lodge and three salvageable cabins must be made habitable. Each structure already had a new roof, but that was it. So much to be done before the long winter set in, both by Cal and herself and local skilled laborers, none of whom seemed prone to speedily working up estimates.

Maggie shook her head and trudged downhill, giving the evil eye to Howie, who was rooting around in a thicket of wild raspberries. She mounted the steps of the lodge, avoiding loose boards, and fetched a beer from the small refrigerator beneath a window in the front room, which she and Cal had claimed as their living quarters. Then she went back outside and followed a rutted track down to the lakeshore, stepping gingerly to avoid the poison ivy that grew in abundance there. A rotted wooden dock tilted over the water; she navigated it as she had the lodge steps and sat down at its end.

Lost Wolf Lake was placid today; on the far side a small motorboat moved slowly, and near the rocky beach to her left a family of mallards floated, undisturbed by human intrusion. Maggie shaded her eyes and scanned the water for the black-and-white loons she'd often spotted in late afternoon, but none was in evidence. The sun sparkled gold against the intense blue. Another day in paradise. . . .

Paradise? Who am I kidding? And what the hell am I doing here?

Well, she'd found the property, hadn't she? Up on a visit last July to Sigrid Purvis, an old college friend who operated an outfitter's business in White Iron—canoe rentals, sportsmen's gear, guided trips to the Boundary Waters. The talk of the town that month had been about old Janice Mott dying and her estate finally putting Sunrise Lodge on the market. Friends of Sigrid's had pretended interest in buying it, just to get a look at a local legend, so she and Maggie decided to take a tour, too.

A tour that Maggie now regarded as her undoing.

At the time, the property had seemed the ideal solution—to Cal's failure to gain tenure and his growing boredom with his work at the University of Minnesota in Minneapolis where he was a professor in the English department. To the empty-nest feeling of their spacious home in St. Paul. To the staleness that had fallen upon their marriage. To her having to deal with clients, mostly housewives, who were too uninventive or uninvolved to decorate their own homes.

Some solution. Now she was one of those housewives, who couldn't even decide on what color to paint a beat-up, water-stained floor in a cabin that one of their two boys—both now in graduate school on the West Coast—might use for a week or so every summer.

But she was not only a housewife, Maggie reminded herself. She was a brush clearer. A demolition expert. A stringer of extension cords. A patcher of chinks between logs. A glazier of broken windows. She could prop up sagging structures. Remove débris from clogged crawl spaces. Empty the chemical toilet. Cook on a propane stove and wash dishes in a cold trickle of water from a five-gallon container.

The house part she could deal with just fine. But the wife part . . . that was another story. She didn't feel like a wife at all any more. The deterioration of her relationship with Cal had been gradual since they'd arrived here at Lost Wolf Lake in April. At first he'd seemed excited about their new life. Then he'd become remote and moody. And then, after he'd taken a bad fall through the rotted floor of one of the cabins, he'd barely spoken to her. Barely made eye contact with her. Barely touched her.

And when he did . . .

Maggie drained her beer and looked out at the center of the lake, where one of the loons had surfaced and was flapping its wings. So free, so joyous. Resembling nothing in her life. Nothing at all.

Because when Cal speaks to me, or looks into my eyes, or accidentally touches me, there's a coldness. A coldness that makes me feel as if he wishes I were dead.

· · ·

The ball game ended—ten to three, Twins—and Abel shut off the TV.

Cal signaled for another Leinie, his third, and the bartender set it in front of him. It was warm in the tavern in spite of the air-conditioning. Cal brushed his thick shock of gray-brown hair off his forehead.

Abel frowned. "Nasty cut you've got there."

Cal fingered it; the spot was scabbed and still tender. "Roof beam fell on me while I was taking down one of the cabins."

"You have it looked at?"

"Not necessary. One of the staples at home is a first-aid kit."

"You must use it a lot." Abel motioned to a burn mark on Cal's right forearm. "Last week it was . . . what? Twisted ankle? And before that a big shoulder bruise."

"Accidents happen."

"You always been accident-prone?"

"No, but I've never done this much physical labor before. Stuff around the house in St. Paul, that's all."

"Told me you'd built a whole addition yourself."

"Well, yeah. But I was a lot younger and more fit then."

"What are you . . . forty-five? Fifty, tops?"

"Forty-six."

"And you still look fit. I'd say you're not keeping your mind on the job at hand. Everything OK out there?"

"What d'you mean?"

"Well, a man who's got problems . . . say, financial or marital . . . can let his concentration slip."

Cal studied Abel Arneson. The man wasn't a friend, not exactly, but he was the first resident of White Iron who'd welcomed Maggie and him, driving out to the lake with a cooler full of freshly caught walleye and two six-packs. He'd steered them to contractors—who had shown up, promised estimates, and someday might call. He'd arranged for the purchase of a used skiff and ten-horsepower Evinrude outboard motor, which were to be delivered this week, and he'd promised to go out with Cal and show him all the best fishing sites. He was the logical person for a worried man to confide in. . . .

Cal said: "To tell the truth, if anything, my concentration's heightened." He paused, sipped beer broodingly. "You see, all these injuries I've had . . . I don't think they were accidental."

When the motorboat was about 100 yards away, Maggie recognized it as Sigrid Purvis's. Sigrid waved, cut back on power, and the boat swung toward the dock—a little too fast, bumping its side and making the rotting timbers groan. As

Maggie went to help Sigrid secure it, Howie ran down the rutted track from the lodge, barking until he recognized the visitor.

Sigrid stepped out of the boat, grinning up at Maggie from under the bill of her Purvis Outfitters baseball cap. She was a tall, thin woman with a wild mane of blonde curls and a weathered face—one made for laughing.

Howie bounded up to her, and she leaned down to pat him, the cap coming loose and nearly falling in the water. Sigrid snatched it up, then reached into the boat and pulled out a plastic sack.

"Blueberries," she said. "My crop's so big I'm getting sick of them."

"Thanks! We could use some fruit. Our raspberries're really tiny, and mainly the birds get them."

"Got a beer?"

"Sure. Come on up."

When they were seated on folding chairs on the lodge's sagging porch, Sigrid said: "Things better or worse with Cal?"

"Worse. The coldness and the silences are really getting to me. And I'm getting vibes off him. Bad ones. Almost as if . . ."

"As if?"

"Forget it."

"Mags, this is Sig you're talking to."

". . . As if he wants to kill me."

"Cal?" Sigrid looked shocked. "That's impossible."

140

"Is it?"

"Of course. Your imagination's in overdrive, is all. Look, you're living on a huge property miles from town. You're both under stress, spending your savings like crazy and trying to get the place in shape before winter sets in. Everything's overgrown, the ruined cabins are creepy, and most of this lodge, except for the front room, is uninhabitable. Cal was depressed at not making tenure to begin with, and now he probably feels this project is more than he can handle. No wonder he's acting weird. And no wonder you're reading all sorts of extreme things into his behavior."

"I wish I could believe that."

"Believe it. It's better than believing he wants to harm you. Or that the place is cursed."

"Cursed?"

"Oh, you know, the local legend. Janice Mott and her husband were having a hard time keeping the lodge going. Old customers dying off, newer ones finding the place too primitive. Then her husband died in a freak accident, and she abandoned the property and moved to that tiny house in town."

"Right. And she never returned here again . . . or allowed anyone else to set foot on the property. Who would, given that kind of tragedy?"

Sigrid was silent for a moment, squinting through the trees at the sliver of lake. "But why not sell it?" she asked. "Why put up an electrified fence and hire a private guard service to patrol it every day? Why, at fifty-five, retreat to that little house in town and never again have contact with anyone, except for random encounters at the grocery and drug stores?"

"The husband's death made her a little crazy?"

"A whole lot crazy, to live in near poverty, paying out all that money to a guard service, while holding on to a prime property like this. And to let it deteriorate the way she did. . . ."

"Maybe I'm beginning to understand her brand of craziness."

Sigrid shook her head. "No, you're not. You've just hit one of those temporary bumps in the road of life. But Janice Mott. . . . It makes you wonder if there's something on this property she didn't want anyone to find."

Abel shook his head. "Professor, if what you say is true, you're in big trouble. But why on earth would Maggie want to kill you?"

"Well, there's a substantial life insurance policy. And our marriage has been pretty much dead for a long time."

"Still, murder. . . . Besides, how would she know to rig those accidents?"

"She worked around contractors in the Twin Cities, knows more than the average person about construction. Easy for her to weaken a floor joist or roof beam, or to cause an electrical fire."

"I just don't buy it."

"I didn't want to believe it, either. But as I told you, each time I've found something that indicated the accident was rigged."

"Wouldn't she be able to hide the evidence?"

"Some things you can't hide."

"I don't know, Professor."

Time to go. Cal stood. "Whether you believe it or not, I want you to remember this conversation. If anything happens to me, repeat it to the police."

On his way out of town, Cal adhered to the speed limit. The local law was strict on speeding, stricter yet on drinking and driving. He didn't want to call attention to himself, not that way.

After Sigrid left to motor back across the lake, Maggie decided to begin clearing out one of the bedrooms. Cal had insisted they make outdoor work and the cabins their priority before it grew cold, and reserve interior work on the lodge for the long snowy winter. But under the circumstances, there was no way she could endure even part of those months living in the single front room; the more space she freed up now, the better she'd survive till springtime.

The bedroom she'd chosen was on the first floor, behind the dining room and kitchen—most likely the former owners' living space, as it connected to another room with a stone fireplace. Both spaces were crammed with heavy dark-wood furniture, probably dating from the late 1940s. The curtains, the rugs, the upholstery, and the mattress had been ravaged by mice and mildew. In the closet, clothing hung in such tatters that it was unrecognizable. The walls were moldy and water-stained, the floorboards buckled.

It's more than I can contend with. Nonsense. Look what you've contended with already.

She began with the bedroom, heaving the mattress from the bed and dragging it through the kitchen—outdated appliances, restaurant-style crockery on sagging shelves, rusting pots and pans on a rack over the stove—and out a side door. The rag rugs and curtains and what remained of the clothing went next. She'd build a pile and hire a hauler who posted on the bulletin board in the supermarket to take it away.

Inside, she looked over the furniture. The bed frame and springs were good; add a new mattress, and it would be a huge step up from the futon in the front room. The bureau's attached mirror had lost much of its silvering; Maggie looked into it, saw herself reflected patchily. In an odd way, she liked the image; she looked the way she felt.

Other than the mirror, the bureau was a fine old piece, and she was sure mice hadn't been able to penetrate its drawers. She began exploring them. The top one on the right was stuck tightly, and it took a few tugs to open it. Inside were a man's possessions: handkerchiefs, a pocket watch, a scattering of miscellaneous cuff links, a ring with a large blue stone, a wallet in its original box, obviously a gift that hadn't been used. The drawer on the left was empty.

The second drawer protruded an inch or so from the ones above and below it. Maggie tugged it open, found a man's clothing: T-shirts, underwear, pajamas. Something *thudded* at the rear, and she pulled the drawer all the way out and removed it.

A blue cloth-bound book. Ledger of some sort.

She flipped back the cover. Not a ledger, a diary, in a woman's back-slanting hand. Blue ink fading but still readable.

April 2, 1948

Our first week here at Lost Wolf Lake! It is so beautiful. I can't believe that John and I had the good fortune to buy the lodge. The owners, who built it in 1913, are old and ill, and made us a very good price. There is a large clientele, and all of the rooms are reserved through the coming season. We've left the guest rooms and the cabins as they were—they have been very well kept up—but I've ordered all new furniture for our suite, and delivery has been guaranteed for tomorrow. I've never kept a diary before now, but from here on out I will, to document our happiness.

Car door slamming below. Cal returning, hours late, with the water and extension cords.

Maggie hesitated only briefly before she shoved the diary back behind the drawer where she'd found it.

"You're limping, Professor. What's the story this time?"

"Bruised foot. I was bringing in some firewood and the pile collapsed on me."

"You been to the hospital?"

"For a bruised foot?"

"Well, I was thinking you ought to be documenting these things that're happening to you. If Maggie is responsible . . ."

"Look, Abel, forget what I told you."

"Thought you wanted me to remember, in case . . ."

"I shouldn't've said the things I did. Nothing's going on out at the lake, except that I'm clumsy. I was in a bad mood and I'd had a few Leinies before I came in here. I talked out of turn."

"But . . ."

"Speaking of Leinies, can I get one, please? And then we'll talk about more pleasant stuff, like the streak the Twins're on."

"Maggie, I think there's something you ought to know."

"Sig! I thought I heard your boat. Help me with

this armchair, will you? The guy's coming to haul the junk away tomorrow."

"It can wait a minute. We have to talk."

"What's wrong? Cal . . . he's not . . . ?"

"So far as I know Cal's fine . . . physically. But mentally . . . I was talking with Abel Arneson at the Walleye Tavern last night. Cal's been spending a lot of time in there on his runs to town."

"I suspected as much. But a few beers, so what?"

"Drinking beer isn't all he's been doing. He's been saying some nasty things to Abel. About you."

"What about me?"

"Cal told Abel . . . he told him you're trying to kill him."

"What?"

"He only talked about it once, over a week ago. Said all these injuries he's sustained lately were your doing. The next time he was in, he claimed he'd had too much to drink and talked out of turn. But Abel doesn't believe him."

"My God! Cal's injured himself a lot, yes, but that's because he's clumsy. He's always been clumsy. Does Abel really believe what he said?"

"He doesn't know what to think."

"Do you believe it?"

"I believe I may have been wrong before. You should watch your back, Mags. You just may be living with a crazy man."

• • •

"I took your advice and went to the hospital this time, Abel. The cut required stitches, and now there's something on record."

"So you've changed your mind about talking."

"Yes. . . . Last time I was in, I was feeling a misguided loyalty to Maggie. All those years, our two boys, et cetera. But this last accident . . . that tore it."

"You've got to look out for yourself."

"From now on, I will."

Maggie took to watching Cal, covertly, through lowered lashes as they worked side-by-side or sat on the porch in the evenings in the light from the mosquito-repellent candles. His gaze was remote, his expression unreadable. But every now and then she'd catch him watching her with the same guarded look she employed.

After a few days, he began working alone on tearing down one of the uninhabitable cabins, encouraging her to complete her renovations of the owners' suite. Grateful for the respite from his oppressive presence, she replaced floorboards and primed walls and refinished the heavy old furnishings. Occasionally she thought of the diary she'd put back where she'd found it behind the second drawer of the bureau. She intended to read more of it, but the work was grueling and made the time go quickly. She told herself she'd save it for the winter months ahead.

Right before the Labor Day weekend, Sigrid reported that she'd seen Cal and Abel Arneson in intense conversation in the Walleye, and that Abel had later refused to tell her what they'd been discussing.

After that, when Cal went out to work alone on the cabins, Maggie covertly followed him. And just as covertly documented his activities.

The roof beam was thick, and, even though the wood was brittle, it was taking Cal a long time to saw through it. He couldn't risk using power tools, though. Maggie wasn't to know about this particular project.

The wind blew off the lake and rustled the branches of the nearby pines. He heard the whine of an outboard motor and Howie's excited barking—probably at the flock of mallards that frequented the water off their dock. The dog had followed him down here to this cabin by what Cal had privately christened Poison Ivy Beach, then wandered off. The mallards were in no jeopardy, though. The damned dog—Maggie's choice, not his—was a lousy swimmer.

Cal hummed tunelessly as he worked. Tomorrow the cabin would be ready.

Maggie crouched behind a thicket of wild raspberries watching as Cal sawed at the beam of the ramshackle cabin. Its front wall had fallen in, so she had a clear view of him. After a moment she activated the zoom lens of her digital camera and took a picture. Last week she'd photographed him deliberately inflicting an axe wound on his arm that had sent him to the emergency room for five stitches. Now it appeared he intended to fake another accident—that of a major support beam dropping on him.

Why is he doing these things to himself? Why is he blaming them on me, telling Abel Arneson I'm trying to kill him? Sigrid said he hasn't spoken to anyone else, or the police. What does he hope to gain from hurting himself?

Just before he'd sawed through the entire beam, Cal used a pair of long metal wedges to brace the beam in place. Each piece had a thin piece of rope tied to it. Then he climbed down the ladder, moved it to its opposite end, climbed back up, and began sawing again.

Maggie documented the activity.

"You look kind of ragged around the edges, Professor."

"I'm not feeling too well tonight. For days, actually."

"How so?"

"Just tired. Haven't been doing too much work out at the property. To tell you the truth, it just doesn't seem to matter any more."

"Thinking of throwing in the towel?"

". . . Yes, I am. The Twin Cities are looking pretty good to me right now. I've just about decided to confront Maggie about what she's been doing, move back, and divorce her."

"But you haven't said anything to her yet?"

"No. God knows what she might do if I did. She'll find out from my lawyer. Besides, she's hardly ever around."

"Oh?"

"Every day she disappears into the woods, down by the beach, where the last few cabins are. Says she needs her space. Damned if I know what she's up to."

"If I were you, Professor, I'd follow her the next time. And do it quietly."

Maggie studied the images on the digital camera's screen, one after the other. Cal sawing one end of the fallen-in cabin's beam; Cal sawing the other; Cal constructing his elaborate system of braces and ropes like trip wires. The braces and ropes themselves, in close-up.

God, I never knew he had such mechanical ability. He's planning another accident . . . a big one this time. The kind that will send him to the hospital. And maybe send me to jail. How did it come to this? He was depressed and acting out against me when he was denied tenure, but the therapy seemed to help. Until we came here. My fault, he'd say. . . .

"Maggie!" His voice, coming from one of the cabins by the beach.

She got up, went to the porch railing, and called: "What is it?"

"I need your help down here."

"Be right with you."

She took the camera into the lodge and set it on the counter. Evidence of Cal's mental instability. *What am I going to do with it?*

"Maggie!"

"Coming!"

Take the image card to a lawyer? The police? Destroy what's left of our marriage? Destroy Cal? I don't love him any more, probably haven't for a long time, but those years together and the boys have to count for something, don't they?

"Maggie!" He wasn't distressed, just insistent.

As she descended the slope to the beach, she took deep breaths, told herself to remain calm.

Cal stood on the ladder inside the cabin, holding the end of the beam that he'd first sawed through yesterday. He was smiling—falsely.

"Sorry to bother you," he said, "but I need you to get up here and hold this for me."

"What?"

"Just climb up and hold it for a minute. You can do that, can't you?"

She pictured the braces and trip wires. Pictured what would happen when everything came tumbling down. And realized what Cal's plan was.

What it had been all along. The knowledge hit her so hard that her gut wrenched.

She fought to control the nausea, said: "Cal, you know I don't like ladders."

"Just for a minute, I promise."

She made her decision and moved toward him. "Just for a minute?" she asked.

"Not even that long."

"OK, if you insist . . . oh my God, look over there!"

She flung her arm out wildly. Cal jerked around. His foot lost purchase on the ladder, and then his hand lost purchase on the beam. He clutched instinctively at one of the ropes. The dilapidated structure came crashing down, taking the ladder and Cal with it.

Maggie's ears were filled with the roar of falling wood and Cal's one muffled cry. Then everything went silent.

Slowly Maggie approached the cabin. Through the rising dust she could see Cal's prone body. His head was under the beam, and blood leaked around the splintered wood. *Dead. As dead as he planned for me to be.*

She fell to her knees on the rocky ground. Leaned forward and retched.

Howie's barking penetrated the silence. After a time Maggie got up shakily, put her hand on his collar, and restrained him from charging at the rubble. She remained where she was, face pressed into the dog's rough coat, until she had the strength to drive to town to notify the police that her husband had had a final, fatal accident.

Five days later, Maggie returned to the lodge for the first time since Cal's body had been taken away by the county coroner's van. Most of the time, until today's inquest, she'd stayed in Sigrid's guest room, unable to sleep, eat, or even communicate her feelings to her old friend. Now it was over.

The verdict had been one of accidental death while attempting to commit a felony. It was the only possible one, given the existence of a large life insurance policy on Maggie's life, taken out at the time she was a partner in an interior design firm, as well as the photographs of Cal inflicting wounds on himself and rigging the cabin. In his testimony, Abel Arneson had said he had doubts about Cal's stories all along: "The professor was an unstable man. Anybody could see that."

So it was over, and she was alone. As alone as Janice Mott had been after her husband died tragically on the property. Janice had fled to town and lived the life of a recluse, but Maggie didn't see that as an option. She didn't even see returning to the Twin Cities as an option. In fact, she saw no options at all.

Howie was whining at the door. She let him out, sat down on the futon couch that folded out into a bed. Stared around the large room and wondered what to do with her life.

Don't think so cosmically. All you have to decide now is what to do tonight. A walk down to the dock? No, too close to where Cal died. Quiet contemplation on the porch? Not that. A book? Couldn't concentrate. Wait . . . there's Janice Mott's diary.

Maggie retrieved it from the bureau drawer where she'd left it.

Janice Mott had kept to her resolve of documenting John's and her happiness at Lost Wolf Lake to the very last day. But the happiness had not lasted. At first the entries had been full of delight and plans for the future. Then Janice's tone changed subtly, with the discovery that she and John were physically incapable of having the family they'd counted on. It grew downbeat as the lodge's clientele eroded, depressed when she realized he was having an affair with a waitress in town. Paranoid as she began to fear John wanted her out of the way so he could marry the woman. And lonely. Very lonely.

May 8, 1970

John is gone so much. When he's not in White Iron with her, he works on the cabins. Getting them ready, he says, for the season. But the guest list is short and most will never be occupied again. For years I've been so wrapped up in him and, in the season, the guests, that I've made no friends. No one to spend time with, no one to confide in.

May 10, 1970
I heard some sawing at the cabin in the pine grove and went there, wondering what John was doing. He was working on the roof beam, and made it clear he didn't want me there. I don't understand. That roof has always been in fine shape. I wish he would stop this needless work and at least spend some time with me.

May 11, 1970
John spent the whole night in town again— with her, of course. He came back this morning and went out to work without an explanation. I think he is ready to leave me, and I don't know what I'll do then.

He's calling out to me now. He says he wants some help. He spends the night in town with her, and now he wants me to help him!

Under this last entry, there was a space, and then the words, scrawled large: *May God have mercy on his—and my—soul!*
Maggie set the journal down. Rested her head on the back of the futon sofa and closed her eyes.
Same acts, different cabins. History repeating

itself? Accidental similarity of events? Or some form of intelligence reaching out from the past? Something in the land itself?

One thing she was sure of—if there ever was a curse, it was gone now. Her future was decided. She was staying.

WRONG PLACE, WRONG TIME

A "Nameless Detective" Story

by Bill Pronzini

Sometimes it happens like this. No warning, no way to guard against it. And through no fault of your own. You're just in the wrong place at the wrong time.

Eleven p.m., drizzly, low ceiling and poor visibility. On my way back from four long days on a case in Fresno and eager to get home to San Francisco. Highway 152, the quickest route from 99 west through hills and valleys to 101. Roadside service station and convenience store, a lighted sign that said *OPEN UNTIL MIDNIGHT.* Older model car parked in the shadows alongside the rest rooms, newish Buick drawn in at the gas pumps. People visible inside the store, indistinct images behind damp-streaked and sign-plastered glass.

I didn't need gas, but I did need some hot coffee to keep me awake. And something to fill the hollow under my breastbone: I hadn't taken the time to eat anything before leaving Fresno. So I swung off into the lot, parked next to the older car. Yawned and stretched and walked past the Buick to the store. Walked right into it.

Even before I saw the little guy with the gun, I knew something was wrong. It was in the air, a heaviness, a crackling quality, like the atmosphere before a big storm. The hair crawled on the back of my scalp. But I was two paces inside by then and it was too late to back out.

He was standing next to a rack of potato chips, holding the weapon in close to his body with both hands. The other two men stood ten feet away at the counter, one in front and one behind. The gun, a long-barreled target pistol, was centered on the man in front; it stayed that way even though the little guy's head was half turned in my direction. I stopped and stayed still with my arms down tightly against my sides.

Time freeze. The four of us staring, nobody moving. Light rain on the roof, some kind of machine making thin wheezing noises—no other sound.

The one with the gun coughed suddenly, a dry, consumptive hacking that broke the silence but added to the tension. He was thin and runty, mid thirties, going bald on top, his face drawn to a drum's tautness. Close-set brown eyes burned with outrage and hatred. The clerk behind the counter, twenty-something, long hair tied in a ponytail, kept licking his lips and swallowing hard; his eyes flicked here and there, settled, flicked, settled like a pair of nervous flies. Scared, but in control of himself. The handsome, fortyish man in front was a different story. He couldn't take his eyes off the pistol, as if it had a hypnotic effect on him. Sweat slicked his bloodless face, rolled down off his chin in little drops. His fear was a tangible thing, sick and rank and consuming; you could see it moving under the sweat, under the skin, the way maggots move inside a slab of bad meat.

"Harry," he said in a voice that crawled and cringed. "Harry, for God's sake . . ."

"Shut up. Don't call me Harry."

"Listen . . . it wasn't me, it was Noreen. . . ."

"Shut up shut up shut up." High-pitched, with a brittle, cracking edge. "You," he said to me. "Come over here where I can see you better."

I went closer to the counter, doing it slowly. This wasn't what I'd first taken it to be. Not a hold-up—something personal between the little guy and the handsome one, something that had come to a crisis point in here only a short time ago. Wrong place, wrong time for the young clerk, too.

I said: "What's this all about?"

"I'm going to kill this son-of-a-bitch," the little guy said, "that's what it's all about."

"Why do you want to do that?"

"My wife and my savings, every cent I had in the world. He took them both away from me and now he's going to pay for it."

"Harry, please, you've got to . . ."

"Didn't I tell you to shut up? Didn't I tell you not to call me Harry?"

Handsome shook his head, a meaningless flopping like a broken bulb on a white stalk.

"Where is she, Barlow?" the little guy demanded.

163

"Noreen?"

"My bitch wife Noreen. Where is she?"

"I don't know. . . ."

"She's not at your place. The house was dark when you left. Noreen wouldn't sit in a dark house alone. She doesn't like the dark."

"You . . . saw me at the house?"

"That's right. I saw you and I followed you twenty miles to this place. Did you think I just materialized out of thin air?"

"Spying on me? Looking through windows? Jesus."

"I got there just as you were leaving," the little guy said. "Perfect timing. You didn't think I'd find out your name or where you lived, did you? You thought you were safe, didn't you? Stupid old Harry Chalfont, the cuckold, the sucker . . . no threat at all."

Another head flop. This one made beads of sweat fly off.

"But I did find out," the little guy said. "Took me two months, but I found you and now I'm going to kill you."

"Stop saying that! You won't, you can't. . . ."

"Go ahead, beg. Beg me not to do it."

Barlow moaned and leaned back hard against the counter. Mortal terror unmans some people; he was as crippled by it as anybody I'd ever seen. Before long he would beg, down on his knees.

"Where's Noreen?"

"I swear I don't know, Harry . . . Mister Chalfont. She . . . walked out on me . . . a few days ago. Took all the money with her."

"You mean there's still some of the ten thousand left? I figured it'd all be gone by now. But it doesn't matter. I don't care about the money any more. All I care about is paying you back. You, and then Noreen. Both of you getting just what you deserve."

Chalfont ached to pay them back, all right, yearned to see them dead. But wishing something and making it happen are two different things. He had the pistol cocked and ready and he'd worked himself into an overheated emotional state, but he wasn't really a killer. You can look into a man's eyes in a situation like this, as I had too many times, and tell whether or not he's capable of cold-blooded murder. There's a fire, a kind of death light, unmistakable and immutable, in the eyes of those who can, and it wasn't there in Harry Chalfont's eyes.

Not that its absence made him any less dangerous. He was wired to the max and filled with hate, and his finger was close to white on the pistol's trigger. Reflex could jerk off a round, even two, at any time. And if that happened, the slugs could go anywhere—into Barlow, into the young clerk, into me.

"She was all I ever had," he said. "My job, my savings, my life . . . none of it meant anything until I met her. Little, ugly, lonely . . . that's all I was. But she loved me once, at least enough to marry me. And then you came along and destroyed it all."

"I didn't, I tell you, it was all her idea. . . ."

"Shut up. It was you, Barlow, you turned her head, you corrupted her. God damn' traveling salesman, god damn' cliché, you must've had other women. Why couldn't you leave her alone?"

Working himself up even more. Nerving himself to pull that trigger. I thought about jumping him, but that wasn't much of an option. Too much distance between us, too much risk of the pistol going off. One other option. And I'd damned well better make it work.

I said quietly, evenly: "Give me the gun, Mister Chalfont."

The words didn't register until I repeated them. Then he blinked, shifted his gaze to me without moving his head. "What did you say?"

"Give me the gun. Put an end to this before it's too late."

"No. Shut up."

"You don't want to kill anybody. You know it and I know it."

"He's going to pay. They're both going to pay."

"Fine, make them pay. Press theft charges against them. Send them to prison."

"That's not enough punishment for what they did."

"If you don't think so, then you've never seen the inside of a prison."

"What do you know about it? Who are you?"

A half truth was more forceful than the whole truth. I said: "I'm a police officer."

Barlow and the clerk both jerked looks at me. The kid's had hope in it, but not Handsome's; his fear remained unchecked, undiluted.

"You're lying," Chalfont said.

"Why would I lie?"

He coughed again, hawked deeply in his throat. "It doesn't make any difference. You can't stop me."

"That's right, I can't stop you from shooting Barlow. But I can stop you from shooting your wife. I'm off duty but I'm still armed." Calculated lie. "If you kill him, then I'll have to kill you. The instant your gun goes off, out comes mine and you're also a dead man. You don't want that."

"I don't care."

"You care, all right. I can see it in your face. You don't want to die tonight, Mister Chalfont."

That was right: he didn't. The death light wasn't there for himself, either.

"I have to make them pay," he said.

"You're already made Barlow pay. Just look at him . . . he's paying right now. Why put him out of his misery?"

For a little time Chalfont stood rigid, the pistol drawn in tightly under his breastbone. Then his tongue poked out between his lips and stayed there, the way a cat's will. It made him look cross-eyed, and for the first time, uncertain.

"You don't want to die," I said again. "Admit it. You don't want to die."

"I don't want to die," he said.

"And you don't want the clerk or me to die, right? That could happen if shooting starts. Innocent blood on your hands."

"No," he said. "No, I don't want that."

I'd already taken two slow, careful steps toward him; I tried another, longer one. The pistol's muzzle stayed centered on Barlow's chest. I watched Chalfont's index finger. It seemed to have relaxed on the trigger. His two-handed grip on the weapon appeared looser, too.

"Let me have the gun, Mister Chalfont."

He didn't say anything, didn't move.

Another step, slow, slow, with my hand extended.

"Give me the gun. You don't want to die tonight. Nobody has to die tonight. Let me have the gun."

One more step. And all at once the outrage, the hate, the lust for revenge went out of his eyes, like a slate wiped suddenly clean, and he brought the pistol away from his chest one-handed and held it out without looking at me. I took it gently, dropped it into my coat pocket.

Situation diffused. Just like that.

The clerk let out an explosive breath, and said—

"Oh, man!"—almost reverently. Barlow slumped against the counter, whimpered, and then called Chalfont a couple of obscene names. But he was too wrapped up in himself and his relief to work up much anger at the little guy. He wouldn't look at me, either.

I took Chalfont's arm, steered him around behind the counter, and sat him down on a stool back there. He wore a glazed look now, and his tongue was back out between his lips. Docile, disoriented. Broken.

"Call the law," I said to the clerk. "Local or county, whichever'll get here the quickest."

"County," he said. He picked up the phone.

"Tell them to bring a paramedic unit with them."

"Yes, sir." Then he said: "Hey! Hey, that other guy's leaving."

I swung around. Barlow had slipped over to the door; it was just closing behind him. I snapped at the kid to watch Chalfont and ran outside after Barlow.

He was getting into the Buick parked at the gas pumps. He slammed the door, but I got there fast enough to yank it open before he could lock it.

"You're not going anywhere, Barlow."

"You can't keep me here. . . ."

"The hell I can't."

I ducked my head and leaned inside. He tried to fight me. I jammed him back against the seat with my forearm, reached over with the other hand, and pulled the keys out of the ignition. No more struggle then. I released him, backed clear. "Get out of the car."

He came out in loose, shaky segments. Leaned against the open door, looking at me with fear-soaked eyes.

"Why the hurry to leave? Why so afraid of me?"

"I'm not afraid of you. . . ."

"Sure you are. As much as you were of Chalfont and his gun. Maybe more. It was in your face when I said I was a cop. It's there now. And you're still sweating like a pig. Why?"

That floppy headshake again. He still wasn't making eye contact.

"Why'd you come here tonight? This particular place?"

"I needed gas."

"Chalfont said he followed you for twenty miles. There must be an open service station closer to your house than this one. Late at night, rainy . . . why drive this far?"

Headshake.

"Must be you didn't realize you were almost out of gas until you got on the road," I said. "Too distracted, maybe. Other things on your mind. Like something that happened tonight at your house, something you were afraid Chalfont might have seen if he'd been spying through windows."

I opened the Buick's back door. Seat and floor

170

were both empty. Around to the rear, then, where I slid one of his keys into the trunk lock.

"No!" Barlow came stumbling back there, pawed at me, tried to push me away. I shouldered him aside instead, got the key turned and the trunk lid up.

The body stuffed inside was wrapped in a plastic sheet. One pale arm lay exposed, the fingers bent and hooked. I pulled some of the sheet away, just enough for a brief look at the dead woman's face. Mottled, the tongue protruding and blackened. Strangled.

"Noreen Chalfont," I said. "Where were you taking her, Barlow? Some remote spot in the mountains for burial?"

He made a keening, hurt-animal sound. "Oh, God, I didn't mean to kill her . . . we had an argument about the money and I lost my head. I didn't know what I was doing . . . I didn't mean to kill her. . . ."

His legs quit supporting him; he sat down hard on the pavement with legs splayed out and head down. He didn't move after that, except for the heaving of his chest. His face was wetter than ever, a mingling now of sweat and drizzle and tears.

I looked over at the misted store window. *That poor bastard in there,* I thought. He wanted to make his wife pay for what she did, but he'll go to pieces when he finds out Barlow did the job for him.

I closed the trunk lid and stood there in the cold, waiting for the law.

Sometimes it happens like this, too. You're in the wrong place at the wrong time, and still things work out all right. For some of the people involved, anyway.

IRREFUTABLE EVIDENCE

A Sharon McCone Story

by Marcia Muller

I tossed the pine cone from hand to hand and looked up at the tree it had fallen from. It was perhaps twenty feet tall and very dense, with branches that swept the ground except on its left-hand side, where they were bent and sheared off. A young bristlecone pine, hundreds of years old and still growing. In the high elevations of California's White Mountains, where the tule elk and wild mustangs range, there are bristlecones over 4,000 years old—some say the oldest living things on the face of the earth. Years ago, I'd made one of the better decisions of my life while lying under such a pine; today, I'd been hoping this tree would yield evidence that would help me identify a killer.

No such luck.

After a time I turned away and, still holding the pine cone, retraced my steps to my rented Jeep. I tossed the cone on the passenger's seat, got in, and cranked up the air conditioning. The temperature was in the mid nineties—August heat. I eased the vehicle over the rocky, sloping ground to the secondary road, bumped along it for two miles, then turned southwest onto Route 168 toward Big Pine, a town of 1,350 nestled in a valley between the Whites and the John Muir Wilderness Area. My motel was on the wide main street, a homey place with a tree-shaded lawn and picnic tables. No high-speed Internet access or other amenities that my operatives at McCone Investigations would have deemed necessities, but plenty good enough for their boss.

I tell my operatives I believe in the simple life. They claim I'm living in the Dark Ages.

Dark Ages, indeed. I had a cell phone, which I took out as soon as I entered my unit and dialed the agency in San Francisco. Ted Smalley, our office manager, sounded relieved when he heard my voice. That morning I'd flown down to Bishop, some fifteen miles north of here, in the Cessna 170B I jointly owned with my significant other, Hy Ripinsky; Ted, ever nervous about what he called my "dangerous hobby," had probably been fretting all day.

"Shar, it's after five o'clock. Where are you?" he asked.

"The motel in Big Pine."

"Why didn't you check in with me from the airport? I've been waiting. . . ."

"There was somebody at the airport who offered me a ride to the dealer I'm renting a car from, so I couldn't take the time. Then I had to stop by the local sheriff's substation to let them know I'd be working in the area, check in here, and . . . why am I explaining all this to you?"

"I don't know. Why are you?"

"Sometimes you remind me of my mother."

"God help me. She's a nice lady, but . . ."

"Yeah. So what's going on there?"

"Quiet day, except for the trouble with the UPS guy."

"Trouble?"

"You don't want to know."

"Probably not. Is Mick in?" Mick Savage, my nephew and chief computer expert.

"No, he left for the day, but he said to tell you he e-mailed the files on the research job you assigned him."

Which I would access on my laptop—another rebuttal to the claim that the boss was living in the Dark Ages.

I read through the files Mick had sent me, then walked down to a steakhouse I'd spotted on the way in. After dinner, I went back to the motel and sat at one of the picnic tables, enjoying the cool of the evening and planning a course of action for the next day. The air was sweet with sage and dry grass; crickets chorused in a field behind the motel, and somewhere far off a dog was barking. I felt relaxed, mellow, even; it was good to get out of the city.

The case I was working had been brought to me by Glenn Solomon, a criminal-defense attorney who threw a lot of business my way. His client, Tom Worthington, had been indicted here in Inyo County for the brutal murder of his lover, Darya

Adams. Worthington was a wealthy man, an olive rancher from over near Fresno; it was natural he would turn to one of the stars of San Francisco's legal community for his defense.

I thought back to the briefing Glenn had given me in his office high atop Embarcadero Four the previous afternoon.

"Tom Worthington is a family man," he'd begun, folding his hands over the well-tailored expanse of his stomach. "Wife, two college-age children. Good reputation. No indications that he's ever strayed before. Darya Adams, he apparently couldn't resist. Former beauty queen . . . Miss California, I believe . . . and widowed. Ran a tourist boutique at Mammoth Lakes. They met when he was on a ski trip there. Before long, they were meeting on a regular basis at a country cabin he bought for her outside Chelsea."

I looked up from the notes I was taking. "Where's Chelsea? I've never heard of it."

"You know Big Pine, Inyo County?"

"As a matter of fact, I do. One of Hy's friends used to have a cabin in the mountains near there."

"Well, Chelsea is a wide place on the road some seven miles into the hills above Big Pine."

"OK, now, the murder . . . ?"

"As close as the medical examiner could pinpoint it, it occurred on July thirty-first. Worthington and Adams had met at the cabin on the twenty-eighth, according to the employee who was minding the boutique in her absence. When Adams didn't return on August first as scheduled, the employee called the cabin, received no answer, then asked the sheriff to check. Place was closed up. On August third, a hiker came across Adams's body in the foothills of the White Mountains several miles from Big Pine. She'd been beaten and strangled. There were signs that the body had been moved there from the place she was killed, but the sheriff's department hasn't been able to determine where that was."

"And they're calling this a crime of passion, perpetrated by your client?"

"Right. One of Darya Adams's friends claimed she was fed up with the arrangement and had threatened to go to his wife if he didn't initiate divorce proceedings. He claims that wasn't true."

"What's the evidence pointing to Worthington?"

Glenn shifted in his chair, reached for the bottled water on the desk.

"Two pieces. One, a key chain near the body, containing a miniature of his Safeway Rewards Club card . . . you know, the ones they give you so, if you lose your keys, whoever finds them can turn them in to the store, and they'll call you. And two, a pine cone in the bed of Worthington's truck."

"A pine cone?"

"A bristlecone, from the tree Adams's body was found under."

179

"How do they know it was from that particular tree?"

"Ah, my friend, that's where it gets interesting. Human beings, as you know, can be identified by their DNA. Animals, too. But are you aware that plants also have DNA?"

"No."

"Well, they do, and, as with humans, the DNA of one plant is unlike the DNA of any other."

"Wait a minute . . . you're saying they ran a DNA test on a pine cone?"

"They did, and it came up a match for those on the tree."

I paused for a moment, letting that sink in. "So what do you expect me to do with this? DNA is a conclusive test."

"Oh, there's no doubt the cone in Tom Worthington's truck came from the place where Darya Adams was found. No doubt it was his key ring near the body. But he insists he's innocent, that she was alive when he left for home the morning of July thirty-first. Says he'd misplaced the key ring at the cabin during a previous visit. Says he doesn't know how the cone came to be in the truck."

"I can see someone planting the keys, but it seems far-fetched that someone would be knowledgeable and clever enough to plant that pine cone."

"Not really. D'you watch any of those true-crime shows on TV?"

"No. They resemble my real life too closely."

"Well, I watch them, and so do millions of others. On July fifteenth, just two weeks before Darya Adams's murder, *Case Closed* did a segment in which a murder conviction hinged on DNA testing of seed pods."

"So someone could've gotten the idea of planting the pine cone from the show?"

"Right."

"And you believe Tom Worthington's being truthful with you?"

"I do. My instincts don't lie."

"That's good enough for me."

"Then what I expect you to do, my friend, should be clear. Find out who left that key ring near the body, and the cone in Worthington's truck. When you do, we'll have our line of defense . . . Darya Adams's real murderer."

As full dark settled in, I returned to my motel room and again looked over the files Mick had sent me. Background on Tom Worthington and Darya Adams. Background on friends and associates, scattered throughout Inyo and Fresno counties. Tomorrow I'd begin interviewing them, starting with those in the Big Pine area, and then visit Worthington at the county jail in Independence.

Finding a lead to Darya Adams's killer wasn't going to be easy. Inyo is California's third largest county—over 10,000 square miles, encompassing mountains, volcanic wasteland, timber, and desert. Its relatively small communities are scattered far and wide. In addition to its size, the county has a reputation for harboring a strange and often violent population. People vanish into the desert; bodies turn up in old mine shafts; bars are shot up by disgruntled customers. It's not uncommon for planes carrying drugs from south of the border to land at isolated airstrips; desert rats and prospectors and cults with bizarre beliefs hole up in nearly inaccessible cañons. I'd have no shortage of potential suspects here.

Too bad my visit to the bristlecone pine under which Darya Adams died hadn't offered a blinding flash of inspiration.

The red sun over the mountains told me the day was going to be hot. I dressed accordingly, in shorts and a tank top, with a loose-weave shirt for protection against the sun. After a big breakfast at a nearby café—best to fortify myself since I didn't know when the next opportunity to eat would present itself—I set off for the offices of Ace Realty, a block off the main street.

According to my background checks, Jeb Barkley, the agent who had handled the sale of the cabin near Chelsea last year, was an old friend of Tom Worthington's, had played football with him at Fresno State. A big man with a round, balding head that looked too small for his body, he was at his desk when I arrived. The other desks were unoccupied and dust-covered; business must not be good.

Barkley greeted me, brought coffee, then sat in his chair, leaning forward, hands clasped on the desk top, a frown furrowing his otherwise baby-smooth brow. "I sure hope you can do something to help Tom, Miz McCone," he said.

"I'm going to try. Did you see him on his last visit?"

"Oh, no. He and Darya . . . they liked their privacy."

"When was the last time you saw him?"

"Couple of months ago. He came alone, to go fishing, and, when he got to the cabin, he discovered he didn't have his keys. So he called me and I drove out to let him in with the spare we keep on file here."

That would support Worthington's claim that he'd misplaced the keys that had been found near Adams's body. "How did he seem?"

"Seem? Oh. . . ." Barkley considered, the furrows in his brow deepening. "I'd say he was just Tom. Cheerful. Glad to be there. He asked if I'd like to go fishing with him, but I couldn't get away."

"Mister Barkley, when Tom Worthington bought the cabin, was it clear to you that he was buying it for Darya Adams?"

"From the beginning. I mean, they looked at a

number of properties together. And the offer and final papers were drawn up in her name, as a single woman."

"As an old friend of Tom's, how did you feel about the transaction?"

"I don't understand."

"Tom Worthington was cheating on his wife. Buying property for another woman. How did that make you feel?"

He hesitated, looking down at his clasped hands. "Miz McCone," he said after a moment, "Tom has had a lot of trouble with his wife. A lot of trouble with those kids of his, too. Darya was a nice woman, and I figured he deserved a little happiness in his life. It wasn't as if he was just fooling around, either. They were serious about each other."

"Serious enough that he would leave his family for her?"

"He said he was thinking of it."

"But so far he hadn't taken any steps toward a divorce?"

"Not that I know of."

"Let me ask you this, Mister Barkley. Are you convinced of Tom Worthington's innocence?"

"I am."

"Any ideas about who might have killed Darya Adams?"

"I've given that some thought. There're a lot of weird characters hanging out in the hills around Chelsea. Screamin' Mike, for one."

"Who's he?"

"Head case, kind of a hermit. Has a shack not too far from Tom and Darya's cabin. Comes to town once a month when his disability check arrives at general delivery. Cashes it at Gilley's Saloon, gets drunk, and then he starts screaming nonsense at the top of his voice. How he got his name."

"Is he dangerous to others?"

"Not so far. Ed Gilley runs him off. He goes back to his shack and sobers up. But you never know."

I made a note about Screamin' Mike. "Anyone else you can think of?"

"There's a cult up one of the cañons . . . Children of the Perpetual Life. Some of their members've had run-ins with the sheriff, and a couple of years ago one of their women disappeared, was never found. Maybe Ed Gilley could help you. Running a saloon, he's hooked in with the local gossip."

I noted the cult's and Gilley's names. "Well, thank you, Mister Barkley," I said. "When I spoke with your local sheriff's deputy yesterday, he told me they have no objection to my examining the cabin, and I have Mister Worthington's permission as well. Has he contacted you about giving me the keys?"

"Yes. But why do you want to go there? If the sheriff's department didn't find anything . . ."

"Even so, there may be something that will give me a lead."

He rose, then hesitated. "The cabin . . . it's kind of hard to find. How about I drive you there, let you in myself?"

At first I balked at the idea, but I sensed a reserve in Jeb Barkley; he might volunteer something useful in a less structured situation. "OK," I said. "I'd appreciate it."

We went outside to a parking area behind the real-estate office, and Barkley unlocked the doors of a blue Subaru Outback whose left side was badly scratched. He saw me looking at it and said: "Damn' kids. Keyed it while the wife and I were at the movies last week."

"I guess kids in small towns aren't any different from those in big cities." I slid into the passenger seat, wincing as the hot vinyl burned the back of my thighs.

"Makes me glad I never had any." Barkley eased his big body behind the wheel.

"You mentioned that Tom Worthington had trouble with his children."

"Yeah. Jeannie, the older one, got into drugs in high school. Tom had her in and out of schools for troubled teens, but it didn't do any good. She's out on her own now, only shows up when she wants money. The boy, Kent, has . . . I guess they call them anger-management problems. Did jail time for beating up his girlfriend. He's in college now and doing well, but Tom says he's still an angry young man."

I made a mental note to find out more about Worthington's troubled offspring. "And his wife . . . what kind of trouble did he have with her?"

". . . I'm not sure I should be talking about that."

"You'll save me from having to ask him."

"Well, OK, then. Betsy, that's the wife's name, she drinks. It's gotten so that she doesn't go out of the house, just drinks from morning till night. Wine after breakfast, the hard stuff in the afternoon, more wine during and after dinner. And then she passes out. They don't have much of a life together."

"Do you think she knew about Darya Adams?"

"Doubt the woman knows much about anything. I mean, when you're in the bag all the time . . ."

"I hear you."

Barkley drove north on the highway for about three miles, then looped off onto a secondary road that twisted and branched, twisted again, and began climbing into the hills between rocky outcroppings to which pines and sage and manzanita stubbornly clung. The road flattened briefly, and a scattering of buildings appeared— grocery store, propane firm, diner, and several small private homes.

"Chelsea," Barkley said, and turned into a side road.

"Not much to it."

"Nope. Of course, it suited Tom and Darya. As I said, they liked their privacy."

"Why here, though? Why didn't they buy a place nearer to Mammoth Lakes, where she had her shop?"

"Darya wasn't comfortable with that. She's . . . she was a prominent businesswoman, active in civic organizations and charities. Until Tom could see his way clear to divorcing Betsy, Darya preferred to keep their relationship secret."

"Exactly why couldn't he see his way clear?"

Barkley glanced at me, lips twisting wryly. "Money . . . what else? Community-property state, lots of assets at stake. He was trying to figure out a way to minimize the divorce's impact on his holdings. I've been advising him how to do that."

"You mean you've been advising him on a way to hide his assets."

Barkley shrugged, turned his eyes back on the road.

After about a mile, he braked and made a sharp right turn into a graveled driveway. Clumps of dry grass stubbled the ground to either side, and ahead, tucked under tall pines and backing up to a rocky hill, stood the cabin. It was small, of stone and logs, with a wide porch running along the front and a dormer window peeking out from under its eaves. Barkley pulled the car up near the steps.

I got out and climbed to the porch. It was refreshingly cool there. Barkley followed, taking out a set of keys, and opened the front door. The interior of the cabin was even cooler.

The main floor was one big room: kitchen with a breakfast bar separating it from an informal dining area, sitting area centering around a stone fireplace. Rustic furnishings, the kind you expect in a vacation place. Stuffed animal heads on the walls; I could feel their glassy eyes watching me.

"Worthington's a hunter?" I asked.

"What? No, the place came furnished."

A spiral staircase led up to a loft. I climbed it, found two bedrooms with a connecting bath. In the larger of the two, the bed was unmade, the blanket and sheets tangled. In the bathroom, towels were draped crookedly over their bars; a silk robe in a red-and-black floral pattern lay on the edge of the tub.

I thought about the vacation place Hy and I owned on the Mendocino coast. At the end of every visit, we took time to tidy it, so we'd be greeted by a clean home when we returned. Tom Worthington claimed he had left the cabin on the morning of July thirty-first—apparently delegating the clean-up to Darya. Darya was due back at her shop in Mammoth Lakes on August first, and she probably would have wanted to go home and get settled in the night before, but there was no sign she'd been preparing to depart. I went down to the kitchen. Dirty dishes were piled in the sink, and a trash receptacle was overflowing. Barkley stood at the counter, his back to me, looking out a greenhouse window.

"Poor hummingbirds," he said. "Their feeder's empty. I think I'll fill it." He reached into a cabinet next to the sink as I went back to the living area.

There were two grass-cloth place mats and pewter salt and pepper shakers on the table, and the chairs had been neatly pushed in. The cushions on the sofa in front of the fireplace were rumpled, but I saw no books, magazines, or anything else of a personal nature. There were no knickknacks, photographs, or pictures on the wall.

Who are you people? I thought, standing by the fireplace. Or, in Darya's case, *who were you?* With the exception of the disarray upstairs and in the kitchen, the cabin might have been a set for a TV movie. I couldn't begin to fathom how the woman had died unless I knew how she had lived. And—with due apologies to Glenn's instincts—I couldn't fully assess Tom Worthington's guilt or innocence until I knew what kind of man he was.

I decided to take a run up Highway 395 to Mammoth Lakes, in Mono County, right away. I'd speak to Adams's employee there. Then, in the afternoon, I'd drive down to the Inyo County jail in Independence.

When Jeb Barkley dropped me off at my rental car, I called the office and asked Mick to start background searches on Tom Worthington's son and daughter. Then I phoned Darya Adams's employee, Kathy Bledsoe, and made an appointment to meet her at Adams's shop, High Desert Mementoes. As I drove northwest on 395, I reviewed what I knew of the woman.

Kathy, according to Mick's files, was an artist, in her mid thirties, around Darya's age. She'd enjoyed some success selling her landscapes through a gallery in Mammoth Lakes. For a number of years she'd been employed as a ski instructor at one of the area's resorts, but had quit in order to devote more time to her painting; it must have been the right move, for a review of a showing of her works at the gallery last year predicted that her career was due to take off.

Mammoth Lakes struck me as an upscale community for Mono County. Hy owned a ranch to the north, near Tufa Lake, that he'd inherited from his stepfather, and I was accustomed to the small towns and open countryside of that area. But here you had good motels (presumably equipped with all the amenities my operatives would find desirable), a variety of restaurants, and shopping centers. A lot of shopping centers. I located Darya Adams's establishment in one of them, not far from 395. Its windows displayed a better class of merchandise than usually found in tourist shops: obsidian sculptures, lava rock, dried desert plants, coffee-table books. The sign on the door said the shop was closed, but when I tapped on the glass, a slender, dark-haired woman admitted me and identified herself as Bledsoe.

When we were seated in a small office behind the selling floor, she said: "Truthfully, I don't know what I can tell you that might help Tom. I mean, I was just here minding the store when Darya . . . Well, I just don't know."

"Basically I'm after background. I take it you knew about Miz Adams's relationship with Mister Worthington?"

"*Knew* about it? I introduced them."

"Tell me about that."

"Tom was a friend of my former husband's. They'd known each other forever, fished together. About two years ago, I had an opening at the Lakes Gallery . . . I'm a painter, landscapes, mainly. Tom was up skiing and came to the show. Darya was there, too. They hit it off, and the rest, as they say, is history." Her dark eyes clouded. "A good history, until last week."

"The relationship was harmonious, then?"

"Very. Darya never mentioned so much as a harsh word."

"So she was open about it with you?"

"Of course. Why d'you ask?"

"I've heard she tried to keep it a secret."

"From people who had no business knowing, yes. But not from me."

"Was Tom planning to divorce his wife?"

"Eventually."

"And Darya had no problem with the delay?"

Kathy Bledsoe smiled faintly. "If anything, she was in favor of waiting. Darya was very independent . . . she'd had to be, since her husband . . . a marine . . . was killed on a military training exercise when she was twenty-three. Darya loved Tom, but I sensed she was having trouble getting used to the idea of giving up some of that independence. The cabin was a sort of compromise for them, a place where they could give living together a trial run."

"Have you ever been to the cabin?"

"Only once. The boutique was closed because some repairs were being done, and Darya wanted to go down to the cabin because she had an appointment with a plumber who was going to install a new hot-water heater. But she didn't want to be there alone, so she asked me along. I had a good time." Bledsoe's eyes filled with tears. "God, it's so damn' unfair!"

I waited till she'd gotten herself under control, then asked: "Why didn't she want to go alone? Because of the isolation?"

"No. Her house here is fairly isolated, and she'd never had a problem with that." Bledsoe frowned. "Now that you mention it, I remember thinking it strange at the time. She seemed on edge the whole time we were there."

Interesting. "Think about that weekend. Did anything unusual happen? Anyone drop by, or call, besides the plumber?"

She thought, shook her head.

"Did Miz Adams ever mention a man called Screamin' Mike?"

"I'm sure I'd remember if she had."

"Anyone else in the area?"

"No."

"But you're sure she was on edge that weekend."

"Yes, I'm sure. Darya was afraid of something or someone down there."

Tom Worthington was a handsome man. Even in the jail jumpsuit, his eyes shadowed and puffy from lack of sleep, his gray-frosted dark hair tousled, he would have turned female heads. We sat in a little visiting room, guard outside, and went over everything he'd told the sheriff's people and Glenn Solomon. Then we went over it again. I found no inconsistencies.

"Mister Worthington," I said, "were you and Miz Adams getting along at the time of her death?"

"Better than ever. That last weekend we spent together was . . . well, I'll never forget it."

"I understand you were planning to leave your wife, marry Miz Adams."

"I had hoped to."

"And the delay was because of your marital situation?"

He rubbed his hand across his stubbled chin, nodded. "My wife . . . has her problems. I was trying to find a way to leave the marriage without exacerbating them."

"She drinks."

". . . Yes. I've been trying to convince her to get help, so has our family doctor. Until she does . . ." He spread his hands.

"I understand. Is your wife the sort of person who becomes violent when she drinks?"

"Betsy? God no! She's constantly sedated."

"Perhaps she's drinking to sublimate anger?"

"I don't . . . oh, I see where you're going. No, Miz McCone, Betsy didn't find out about Darya and kill her. She hasn't left the house, except when I've forced her to accompany me, in five years. And those occasions were not successful ones."

"What about your children . . . did they know about your affair with Miz Adams?"

"Jeannie, my daughter, didn't. She's too caught up in her drugged-out little world. Kent did. He's visited at the cabin, and he liked Darya. She had a calming effect on him."

"I understand he has anger-management problems."

"Yes. Anger toward his mother, primarily. But he's working on them."

"Mister Worthington, are you aware that Miz Adams was afraid of something or someone? And that it was connected with your cabin?"

"Darya? Afraid?"

I explained what Kathy Bledsoe had told me.

Worthington shook his head in a bewildered way. "Why didn't she confide in me? Or in Jeb? If somebody'd been bothering her while she was down there, he would've taken care of them."

"Jeb's a good friend?"

"The best. He'd do anything for me. Or Darya."

"He claims he was advising you on how to conserve your assets in the event of a divorce."

Worthington had been grim-faced through most of our meeting, but now he smiled. "Jeb? He's the one who needs advice when it comes to financial matters."

"Why d'you say that?"

"Jeb nearly lost his shirt in a real-estate deal a couple of years ago. High risk, and I warned him not to get into it, but he wouldn't listen. Now he's got a big balloon payment coming due, and he can't cover it. Jeb's a sweet guy, but . . ." He spread his hands. "He introduced Darya and me, you know."

"I thought Kathy Bledsoe did."

"We deliberately gave her that impression. I went up to meet Darya at an opening at the Lakes Gallery . . . turned out Kathy was the artist. I was taken aback to see an old acquaintance, and find out she worked for Darya. Darya sensed my discomfort and played along when Kathy introduced us. But no, I met Darya about six months before that at Jeb's house in Big Pine."

"And how long had Jeb known her?"

"His whole life. Darya was his cousin."

"No, Shar," Mick said over the phone. "Jeb Barkley has no cousin. And neither does Darya Adams."

"Are you sure?"

"My computer doesn't lie."

"Why not? Mine does, all the time."

"That's because you don't use the right databases."

That was probably true. I sighed.

"Shar? Anything else?"

"Yes. I need deep background on Jeb Barkley and Darya Adams. Specifically, if either has a criminal record."

The scenario that came together in my mind as I drove back to Big Pine was a disturbing one. Jeb Barkley had no cousin; Darya Adams had none, either. But Tom Worthington was under the impression they were related.

Barkley had introduced Adams to him as his cousin. Why?

Wealthy man with an unhappy home life. Young, attractive single woman. Old friend who has lost money in a real-estate deal and has a large balloon payment coming up in a year and a half. He introduces the woman as his cousin. The wealthy man is induced to leave his wife for her. The woman then has a community-property stake in those assets . . . which she can share with her "cousin."

Not cousins—partners in crime.

But something had gone wrong.

My phone buzzed. I pulled to the side of the road, picked up. Mick.

"Shar, I called Adah Joslyn at the SFPD."

Adah, an inspector on the Homicide detail, and a good friend. "And?"

"She accessed Barkley's and Adams's criminal records for me. The two of them . . . Adams was Darya Dunn then, her maiden name before she married the marine . . . were arrested over in Nevada fifteen years ago on a bunko charge. Barkley did time. From what I'm reading between the lines, he took the rap for Adams."

"Why didn't this show up in your original backgrounding?"

A silence. Then, reproachfully: "You didn't specify deep backgrounding, Shar. Criminal records're hard to access unless you want to use contacts like Adah. And you've warned me not to abuse the privilege."

I sighed. "Well, it didn't occur to me to go deep on an old friend who sold them a house . . . or on the victim."

"Which leads us to private investigator's lesson number one . . ."

"Right. Suspect everyone." I thanked Mick and broke the connection. Pulled back onto the road.

Jeb Barkley finds his former partner in crime running a boutique up in Mammoth Lakes. He needs money badly, and his friend Tom Worthington has refused to help him out. Darya is attractive, just the sort of woman who might attract a man like Worthington, who is trapped in a dead marriage. So Barkley reminds Adams of the old days and puts pressure on her to begin a relationship with Worthington, with an eye to getting her hands on his assets. Adams agrees, because she values her reputation and position in her community. But then Adams and Barkley have a falling out, maybe because she'd actually fallen in love with her victim. Now she's afraid of someone down at the cabin.

Barkley, who demonstrated this morning that he was familiar with the place—so much so that he even knew where she kept the hummingbird food—and who also had a set of keys.

And she'd had good reason to be afraid. He'd found her alone on July thirty-first, they'd quarreled, and he'd killed her. Then he'd planted evidence to implicate his friend.

Now what I needed was concrete evidence to implicate him.

As I drove the rest of the way to Big Pine, I kept

thinking about the tree that Darya Adams's body had been found under. On impulse, when I reached the intersection of Routes 395 and 168, I turned east into the foothills.

The bristlecone stood alone on the rocky slope, clinging to the poor, coarse soil. I got out of the Jeep and walked around it, ducked under its low-hanging branches. Even though the sun was dipping below the ridge to the west, it felt uncomfortably warm there, and the air was dusty enough to make me sneeze. I went out the other side where the branches were bent and sheared off, sap congealing on their broken tips.

Emergency vehicles, I thought. They did this damage getting the body out.

Or . . . ?

I took out my cell phone, called the local sheriff's department substation. The officer I'd spoken with the previous afternoon, who had been one of the first at the murder scene, took a look at the official photographs and confirmed my suspicion.

"Our people did some damage after the photos were taken," he told me, "but the tree was already ripped up on that side, probably by your client's truck when he dumped the body."

"Was there damage to Mister Worthington's truck? Chipped paint, scratches?"

A pause. "I don't see any photos or mention of it."

"In your opinion, if his truck was scratched, would the paint contain traces of the tree's DNA?"

"Well, I'm not a lab technician, Miz McCone, but I'll hazard a guess that it would."

"Thanks. I'll be in touch."

Jeb Barkley's house was on a quiet side street in Big Pine: a small stucco bungalow on a small lot with a patch of lawn out front. A sprinkler was throwing out lazy arcs of water, and light glowed behind blinds in the windows. Barkley's Outback stood before the closed doors of a single-car garage. I parked down the block and waited until it was fully dark before I approached.

Armed with a paint scraper and one of the plastic bags I'd earlier purchased at a hardware store, I crept up to the passenger side of the car. I switched on my pencil flashlight and, holding it between my teeth, began removing flecks of paint from the scratched area on the door. When I had a respectable amount, I sealed the bag.

I glanced at the house. No visible activity there. Slowly I began to move around the car, shining the beam over it. Nothing distinctive about the tires—and the sheriff's people hadn't been able to take any impressions at the scene, anyway. A few more scratches on the front panel, nothing lodged under the bumper.

The outside vent below the windshield, maybe. He would have removed anything obvious that was caught there, probably had washed the car, but deep down inside . . .

Yes!

I glanced over at the house. Still no activity. I fumbled in my bag for the pouch where I keep miscellaneous objects—chopstick, nail clippers, tweezers for the splinters I'm always getting. Took out the tweezers and fished around in the vent, until I found a slender wood fragment.

Ten to one it came from the bristlecone pine. There was another fragment lodged down there, but I'd leave it for the sheriff's technicians.

I slipped back to the Jeep, headed for the substation.

Overconfidence, I thought, that's what always brings them down. Jeb Barkley hadn't counted on anyone looking into his past and discovering his connection with Darya Adams. He hadn't bothered to have his car repainted because who would suspect him—a small-town real-estate agent, and Tom Worthington's friend—of killing anyone? He hadn't even bothered to conceal from me his knowledge of where things were kept in the cabin.

All of that, and irrefutable DNA evidence as the clincher.

Glenn Solomon was going to love this. Maybe he'd even pay a bonus for my getting results in record time.

THE CARVILLE GHOST

A John Quincannon Story

by Bill Pronzini

Sabina said: "A ghost?"

Barnaby Meeker bobbed his shaggy head. "A strange apparition of unknown origin, Missus Carpenter. I've seen it with my own eyes more than once."

"In Carville, of all places?"

"In a scattering of abandoned cars near my home there. Floating about inside different ones and then rushing out across the dunes."

"How can a group of abandoned horse-traction cars possibly be haunted?"

"How, indeed?" Meeker said mournfully. "How, indeed?"

"And you say this apparition fled when you chased after it?"

"Both times I saw it. Bounded away across the dune tops and then simply vanished into thin air. Well, into heavy mist, to be completely accurate."

"What did it look like, exactly?"

"A human shape surrounded by a whitish glow. Never have I seen a more eerie and frightening sight."

"And it left no footprints behind?"

"None. Ghosts don't leave footprints, do they?"

"*If* it was a ghost."

"The dune crests were unmarked along the thing's path of flight and it left no trace in the cars . . . except, that is, for claw marks on the walls and floors. What else could it be?"

Quincannon, who had been listening to all of this with a stoic mien, could restrain himself no longer. "Balderdash," he said emphatically.

Sabina and Barnaby Meeker both glanced at him in a startled way, as if they'd forgotten he was present in the office.

"Glowing apparitions, sudden disappearances, unmarked sand . . . confounded claptrap, the lot." He added for good measure: "Bah!"

Meeker was offended. He drew himself up in his chair, his cheeks and chest both puffing like a toad's. "If you doubt my word, sir . . ."

It's not your word I doubt but your sanity, Quincannon thought, but he managed not to voice the opinion. "There are no such beings as ghosts," he said.

"Three days ago I would have agreed with you. But after what I've seen with my own eyes . . . my own eyes, I repeat . . . I am no longer certain of anything."

Sabina stirred behind her desk. Pale March sunlight, slanting in through the windows that faced on Market Street, created shimmering highlights in her upswept black hair. It also threw across the desk's polished surface the shadow of the words painted on the window glass: *Carpenter and Quincannon, Professional Detective Services.*

She said: "Others saw the same as you, Mister Meeker?"

"My wife, my son, and a neighbor, Artemus Crabb. They will vouchsafe everything I have told you."

"What time of night did these events take place?"

"After midnight, in all three cases. Crabb was the only one who saw the thing the first time it appeared. I happened to awaken on the second night and spied it in one of the cars. I went out alone to investigate, but it fled and vanished before I could reach the cars. Lucretia, my wife, and my son Jared both saw it last night . . . in one of the cars and then on the dune tops. Jared and I examined the cars by lantern light and again in the morning by daylight. The marks on walls and floor were the only evidence of its presence."

"Claw marks, you said?"

Meeker repressed a shudder. "As if the thing had the talons of a beast."

Quincannon said: "And evidently the heart of a coward."

"Sir?"

"Why else would it run away or bound away or whatever it did? It's humans who are afraid of ghosts, not the converse."

"I have no explanation for what happened," Meeker said. "That is why I have come to you."

"And just what do you expect us to do? Missus

Carpenter and I are detectives, not dabblers in paranormal twaddle."

Again Meeker puffed up. He was an oddly shaped gent in his forties, with an abnormally large head set on a narrow neck and a slight body. A wild tangle of curly hair made his head seem even larger and more disproportionate. He carried a blackthorn walking stick, which he held between his knees and thumped on the floor now and then for emphasis.

"What I want is an explanation for these bizarre occurrences. Normal or paranormal, it matters not to me, as long as they are explained to my satisfaction. If they continue and word gets out, residents will leave and no new ones come to take their place. Carville will become a literal ghost town."

"And you don't want this to happen."

"Of course not. Carville-by-the-Sea is my home and one day it will be the home of many other progressive-minded citizens like myself. Businesses, churches . . . a thriving community. Why, no less a personage than Adolph Sutro hopes to persuade wealthy San Franciscans to buy land there and build grand estates like his own at Sutro Heights."

A cracked filbert, Mister Barnaby Meeker, Quincannon thought. Anyone who chose of his own free will to live in a home fashioned of abandoned street cars in an isolated, wind-and-sand-blown, fog-ridden place like Carville was welcome to the company of other cracked filberts, Adolph Sutro and his ilk included. He had no patience with eccentrics of any stripe, a sentiment he had expressed to Sabina on more than one occasion. She allowed as how that was because he was one himself, but he forgave her. Dear Sabina—he would forgive her anything. Except, perhaps, her steadfast refusal to succumb to his advances. . . .

"I will pay you five hundred dollars to come to Carville and view the phenomenon for yourself," Barnaby Meeker said.

"Eh? What's that?"

"Five hundred dollars, sir. And an additional one thousand dollars if you can provide a satisfactory explanation for these fantastic goings-on."

Quincannon's ears pricked up like a hound's. "Fifteen hundred dollars?"

"If, as I said, you provide a satisfactory explanation."

"Can you afford such a large sum, Mister Meeker?"

"Of course I can afford it," Meeker said, bristling. "Would I offer it if I couldn't?"

"Ah, I ask only because . . ."

"Only because of where I choose to reside." Meeker thumped his stick to punctuate his testy displeasure. "It so happens I am a man of considerable means, sir. Railroad stock, if you must know . . . a substantial portfolio. I have made my home in Carville because I have always been fond of the ocean and the solitude of the dunes. Does that satisfy you?"

"It does." Quincannon's annoyance and suspicion had both vanished as swiftly as the alleged Carville ghost. A smile now bisected his freebooter's beard, the sort Sabina referred to rather unkindly as his "greedy grin." "I meant no offense. You may consider us completely at your service."

"John," Sabina said, "let's not be hasty. You know how busy we are. . . ."

"Now, now, my dear," he said, "Mister Meeker has come in good faith with a vexing problem. We can certainly find the time and wherewithal to oblige him."

"And naturally you'll keep an open mind in the process."

Quincannon chose to ignore her mocking tone. He rose, beamed at the cracked filbert, shook his hand with enthusiasm, and said: "Now, to business. . . ."

When Barnaby Meeker had gone, leaving a $500 check neatly blotted on Sabina's desk, she said: "I'm not so sure it was a good idea to take on this case."

"No? And why not, with five hundred dollars in hand and another thousand promised?"

"We've a full plate already, John. Or have you

forgotten the pickpocket case, the missing Miss Devereaux, and the Wells Fargo Express robbery?"

"Hardly. You'll identify the amusement park dip, we'll find Miss Devereaux, and I have no doubt I'll locate the Wells Fargo bandits and recover the stolen loot before anyone else can . . . all in good time." Quincannon rubbed his hands together briskly and opined: "This ghost foolishness can be disposed of in short order tonight. Fifteen hundred dollars is a handsome fee for a few hours' easy work."

"Don't be too sure it will be easy. Or that it's foolishness."

"Of course it is," he said. "Ghoulies, ghosties, things that go bump in the night. Pure hogwash."

Late that afternoon, huddled inside his greatcoat, Quincannon drove the hired livery horse and buggy out past Cliff House and Sutro Heights. A chill, southwesterly wind blew curls and twists of fog in off the Pacific; the mist was already thick enough to hide the sea from the road, although he could hear the distant murmur of surf and the barking of sea lions. The foghorn on the Potato Patch off Point Lobos gave off its mournful moan at regular intervals.

This was a bleak, lonesome section of the city, sparsely traveled beyond the Heights. As he rattled past the Ocean Boulevard turning into

Golden Gate Park, a lone wagon emerged from the jungle-like tangle of scrub pine and manzanita that marked the park's western edge; otherwise, he saw no one. Empty sand-blown roadway, grass-topped dunes, gulls, fog—a blasted wasteland. There were no lampposts here, south of the park. At night, in heavy fog, the highway was virtually impassable, even with the strongest of lanterns, to all but the blind and the foolhardy.

The sea mist thinned and thickened at intervals until he reached Carville, where it roiled in like a ragged gray shroud spread out over the barren dunes. Carville-by-the-Sea. *Faugh.* Some name for a scattering of weather-rusted streetcars and cobbled together board shacks that had been turned into habitations of one type or another by filberts such as Barnaby Meeker.

San Francisco's transit companies were the culprits. When the city began replacing horse-drawn cars with cable cars and electric streetcars, some of the obsolete carriages had been sold to individuals for $10 if the car had no seats, $20 if it did; the rest were abandoned out here among the dunes, awaiting new buyers or to succumb to rust and rot in the salty sea winds. A grip man for the Ellis Street line had been the first to see the nesting possibilities; in 1895, after purchasing a lot near the terminus of 20th Avenue, he had joined three old North Beach & Mission horse cars and mounted them on stilts above the shifting sand. The edifice was still standing three years later; Quincannon had passed it on the way, a lonesome sight half obscured by the blowing mist.

Farther south, where the Park and Ocean railway line terminated, a Civil War vet named Colonel Charles Daily made his home in a shell-decorated realtor's shed. An entrepreneur, Daily had bought three cars and rented them at $5 each—one to a ladies' bicycle club known as The Falcons—and also opened a coffee saloon. Others, Barnaby Meeker among them, bought their own cars and set them up in the vicinity. A reporter for the *Bulletin* dubbed the place Beachside, but residents preferred Carville-by-the-Sea and the general public shortened that to Carville.

Quincannon had been there before, once on an outing with a young woman of his acquaintance, once on the trail of a thief who had used the rag-tag community as a temporary hide-out before taking it on the lammas to San Jose. It had grown since his last visit over a year ago. Most of the structures were strung closely together along the highway, a few others spaced widely apart among the seaward dunes. Most were more or less permanent homes—single or double-stacked cars, some drawn together in horseshoe shapes for protection against the wind, and embellished by lean-tos and fenced porches. A few were part-time dwellings—clubhouses, weekend retreats or, by reputation, rendezvous for lovers. The whole had a colorless, wind-blown, sanded appearance that blue sky and sunlight did little to brighten; on days like this one, it was downright dismal.

The coffee saloon, a single car with a slant-roofed portico, bore a painted sign: *The Annex*. Smoke dribbled out of its chimney, to be snatched away immediately by the wind. Quincannon pulled the buggy off the road in front, affixed the weighted hitch strap to the horse's bit, and went inside.

It was a rudimentary place, with a narrow foot-railed counter running most of its width. There were no seats or decorations of any kind. The smells of strong-brewed coffee and pitch pine burning in a potbellied stove were welcome after the long, cold ride from downtown.

The counterman was a stooped oldster with white whiskers and tufts of hair that grew patchily from his scalp like saw grass atop the beach dunes. Quincannon sensed immediately that he was the garrulous type hungry for company and this proved to be the case.

"One coffee coming up," the oldster said, and, as he served it in a steaming mug: "Colder than a witch's hind end out there. My name's Potter, but call me Caleb, ever'body does. Passing by or visiting, are ye?"

"John Quincannon. Visiting."

"Ye don't mind me asking who?"

"The Barnaby Meekers."

"Nice folks, Mister and Missus Meeker. The boy's a mite rascally, but then so was I at his age. You a friend of theirs?"

"A business acquaintance of Mister Meeker." Quincannon sugared his coffee, found it too strong, and added another spoonful. "Strange goings-on out here of late, I understand," he said conversationally.

"How's that? Strange goings-on?"

"Ghost lights in cars and vanishing spooks in the dunes."

"Oh, that," Caleb said. "Mister Meeker told you, I expect."

"He did."

"Well, I ain't one to dispute a man like Barnaby Meeker, nor any other man with two good eyes, but it's a tempest in a teapot, ye ask me."

"You haven't seen these apparitions yourself, then?"

"No, and nobody else has, neither, except the Meekers and a fella name of Crabb. Neighbor of theirs out there in the dunes." Caleb leaned forward and said confidentially, even though there was no one else in the car: "Just between you and me, I wouldn't put too much stock in what Mister Crabb says on the subject."

"Why is that?"

"Well, he's kind of a queer bird. Wouldn't think it to look at him, as strapping as he be, but he's

215

scared to death of the supernatural. Come in here the morning after he first seen the will-o'-the-wisp or whatever it was and he was white as a ghost himself. Asked me all sorts of questions about spooks and such, whether we'd had 'em out here before. I told him no and 'twas likely somebody out with a lantern, or his eyes playing tricks, but he was convinced he seen the ghost two nights in a row." Caleb chuckled, revealing loose-fitting store-bought teeth. "Some folks is sure gullible."

"He lives alone, does he?" Quincannon asked.

"Yep. Keeps to himself, don't have much truck with any of the rest of us. Only been living in Carville a couple of weeks or so. Squatter, unless I miss my guess. I can spot 'em, the ones just move in all of a sudden and take over a car without paying for the privilege."

"What does he do for a living?"

"He never said. Mister Meeker's boy Jared says he's a construction worker, but seems to me he don't go nowhere much during the day."

"Jared Meeker knows him, then."

"To pass the time of day with. Seen 'em doing that once."

Quincannon finished his coffee, declined a refill, and went out to the rented buggy. The branch lane that led to the Meekers' home was 200 rods farther south. The buggy alternately bounced and slogged along the sandy surface; once, a hidden rut lifted Quincannon off the seat and made him pull back hard enough on the reins nearly to jerk the horse's head through the martingale loops. Neither this nor the cold wind or the bleakness dampened his spirits. A few minor discomforts were a small price to pay for a $1,500 fee.

The lane led in among the dunes, dipped down into a hollow where it split into two forks. A driftwood sign mounted on a pole there bore the name Meeker and an arrow pointing along the right fork. In that direction Quincannon could see a group of four traction cars, two set end to end, the others at a right and a left angle at the far ends, like an arrangement of dominoes; mist-diffused lamplight showed faintly behind curtained windows in one of the two middle cars. A way down the left fork stood a single car canted slightly against the dune behind it; some distance beyond, eight or nine abandoned cars were jumbled together among the sandhills as if tossed there by a giant's hand. Thick tendrils of fog gave them an insubstantial, almost ethereal aspect, one that would be enhanced by darkness and imagination. A ghost's lair, indeed.

Quincannon left the buggy at the intersection of the two lanes, ground-hitched the horse, and trudged through drifted sand along the left-hand fork. No lights or chimney smoke showed in the single canted car; he by-passed it and continued on to the jumble.

From the outside there was nothing about any of

the abandoned cars to catch the eye. They were or had been painted in various colors, according to which transit company owned them; half had been there long enough for the colors to have faded entirely and the metal and glass surfaces to become sand-pitted. Three had belonged to the Market Street Railway, four to the Ferries and Cliff House Railway, the remaining two to the California Street Cable Railroad.

Quincannon wound his way among them. No one had prowled here recently; the sand was wind-scoured to a smoothness that bore no footprints or anything other than tufts of saw grass. He trudged back to the nearest one, stepped up and inside. All the seats had been removed; he had a brief and unpleasant feeling of standing inside a giant steel coffin. There was nothing in it other than a dusting of sand that had blown in through the open doorway. And no signs that anyone had been inside since it was discarded.

He investigated a second car, then a third. These, too, had had their seats removed. Only the second contained anything to take his attention—faint scuff marks in the drifted sand, the fresh claw-like scratches on walls and floor that Barnaby Meeker had alluded to. The source and meaning of the scratches defied accurate guessing. He stepped outside, with the intention of entering the next nearest car—and a man appeared suddenly from around the end of the car, stood glowering with his hands fisted on his hips and his legs spread, and demanded: "Who are you? What're you doing here?"

Without replying, Quincannon took his measure. He was some shy of forty, heavily black-whiskered but bald on top, with thick arms and hips broader than his shoulders. The staring eyes were the size and color of blackberries. The man seemed edgy as well as suspicious. None of this was as arresting as the fact that he wore a holstered revolver, the tail of his coat swept back, and his hand on the weapon's gnarled butt—a large-bore Bisley Colt, judging from its size.

"Mister, I asked you who you are and what you're doing here."

"Having a look around. My name's Quincannon. And you, I expect, would be Artemus Crabb."

"How the devil d'you know my name?"

"Barnaby Meeker mentioned it."

"Is that so? Meeker a friend of yours?"

"Business acquaintance."

"That still don't explain what you're doing poking around these cars."

"I'm thinking of buying some of them," Quincannon lied glibly.

"Why?"

"For the same reason you and Meeker bought yours. You did buy yours, didn't you?"

Crabb's glower deepened. "Who says I didn't?"

"A curious question, my friend, that's all."

"You're damn' curious about everything, ain't you?"

"It's my nature." Quincannon smiled. "Ghosts and goblins," he said then.

"What?" Crabb jerked as if he'd been struck. The hand hovering above the holstered Bisley shook visibly. "What're you talking about?"

"Why, I understand these cars are haunted. Fascinating, if true."

"It ain't true! Ain't no such things as ghosts!"

"It has been my experience that there are. Oh, the tales I could tell you of the spirit world and its evil manifestations. . . ."

"I don't want to hear it. I don't believe none of it," Crabb said, but it was plain that he did. And that the prospect frightened him as much as Caleb Potter had indicated.

"Mister Meeker tells me you've seen the apparition that inhabits these cars. Dancing lights, a glowing shape that races across the tops of dunes, and then vanishes, poof, without a trace. . . ."

"I ain't gonna talk about that. No, I ain't!"

"I find the subject intriguing," Quincannon said. "As a matter of fact, I'm hoping there is a ghost and that it occupies the very car I purchase. I'd welcome the company on a dark winter's night."

Crabb said something that sounded like—"Gah!"—and turned abruptly and scurried away. At the end of the car he stopped, looked over his shoulder, and called out: "You know what's good for you, you stay away from these cars. Stay away!" Then he was gone into the swirling mist.

Quincannon finished his canvas of the remaining cars. Two others showed faint footprints and scratch marks on the walls and floor. In the second his keen eye picked out something half buried in drifted sand in one corner—a small but heavy piece of metal with a tiny ring soldered onto one end. After several turns in his hand, he identified it as a fisherman's lead sinker. He studied it for a few seconds longer, then pocketed it and left the car.

Before he quit the area he climbed up to the top of the nearby line of dunes. Thick salt grass and stubby patches of gorse grew on the crests; the sand there was windswept to a tawny smoothness, without marks of any kind except for the imprint of Quincannon's boots as he moved along. From this vantage point, through intermittent tears in the curtain of fog, he could see the white-capped ocean in the distance, the long beach and line of surf that edged it. The distant roar of breakers was muted by the wind's wail.

He walked for some way, examining the surfaces. There was nothing up here to take his eye. No prints, no mashing of the grass or gorse to indicate passage. The steep slopes that fell away on both sides were likewise smoothly scoured, barren but for occasional bits of driftwood.

Wryly he thought: *Whither thou, ghost?*

• • •

The Meeker property was larger than it had seemed from a distance. In addition to the domino-styled home, there were a covered woodpile, a cistern, a small corral and lean-to built with its back to the wind, and on the other side of the cars a dune-protected privy. As Quincannon drove the buggy up the lane, Barnaby Meeker came out to stand, waiting, on a railed and slanted walkway fronting the two center cars. A thin woman wearing a woolen cape soon joined him. Meeker gestured to the lean-to and corral, where an unhitched wagon and a roan horse were picketed and where there was room for the rented buggy and livery plug. Quincannon debouched there, decided he would deal with the animal's needs later, and went to join Meeker and the woman.

She was his wife, it developed, given name Lucretia. Her handshake was as firm as a man's, her eyes bird-bright. She might have been comely in her early years, but she seemed to have pinched and soured as she aged; her expression was that of someone who had eaten one too many sacks full of lemons. And she was not pleased to meet him.

"A detective, of all things," she said. "My husband can be foolishly impulsive at times."

"Now, Lucretia," Meeker said mildly.

"Don't deny it. What can a detective do to lay a ghost?"

"If it is a ghost, nothing. If it isn't, Mister Quincannon will find out what's behind these . . . will-o'-the-wisps."

"Will-o'-the-wisps? On foggy nights with no moon?"

"Whatever they are, then."

"Your neighbor believes it's a genuine ghost," Quincannon said. "If you'll pardon the expression, the incidents have him badly spooked."

"You saw Mister Crabb, did you?" Meeker asked.

"I did. Unfriendly gent. He warned me away from the abandoned cars."

"Good-for-nothing, if you ask me," Mrs. Meeker said.

"Indeed? What makes you think so?"

"He's a squatter, for one thing. And he has no profession, for another. No licit profession, I'll warrant."

"According to the counterman at the coffee saloon, Crabb told your son he was in construction work."

"Jared, you mean?" Her mouth turned even more lemony. "Another good-for-nothing."

"Now, Lucretia," Meeker said, not so mildly.

"Well? Do you deny it?"

"I do. He's yet to prove himself, that's all."

"Never will, I say."

The Meekers glared at each other. Mrs. Meeker was victorious in the game of stare down—as she would be most times they played it, Quincannon thought. Her husband averted his gaze and said to Quincannon: "Come inside. It's nippy out here."

The end walls where the two cars were joined had been removed to create one long room. It seemed too warm after the outside chill; a potbellied stove glowed cherry-red in one corner. Quincannon accepted the offer of a cup of tea and Mrs. Meeker went to pour it from a pot resting atop the stove. He managed to maintain a pokerface as he surveyed the surroundings. The car was a combination parlor, kitchen, and dining area, but it was like none other he had ever seen or hoped to see. The contents were an amazing hodge-podge of heavy Victorian furniture and decorations that included numerous framed photographs and daguerreotypes, gewgaws, gimcracks, and what was surely flotsam that had been collected from the beaches—pieces of driftwood, odd-shaped bottles, glass fisherman's floats, a section of draped netting like a moldy spider web. The effect was more that of a junk shop display than a comfortable habitation.

"Your son isn't home, I take it," Quincannon said. The tufted red-velvet chair he perched on was as uncomfortable as it looked.

"Thomas is a sergeant in the United States Army," Mrs. Meeker said. "Stationed at Fort Huachuca. We haven't seen him in two years, to my sorrow."

Meeker said—"Thomas is our eldest son."—and added wryly: "My wife's favorite, as you may have surmised."

"And why shouldn't he be? He's the only one who has amounted, or will amount, to anything."

"Now, Lucretia"—with bite in the words this time—"the way you malign Jared is annoying, to say the least. He may be a bit wild and irresponsible, but he . . ."

"A bit wild and irresponsible? A bit!" The teacup rattled in its saucer, spilling hot liquid that Quincannon barely managed to avoid, as she handed him the crockery. "He's a young scamp and you know it . . . worse today than when he was a kiting youngster. Up and quit the only decent job he ever held just last week, after less than a month's honest labor."

Quincannon cocked a questioning eyebrow at his employer.

"It was a clerk's job downtown, and poorly paid," Meeker said. "He's a bright lad and he'll find a more suitable position one day, . . ."

"You won't live long enough to see the day and neither will I."

"That's enough, Lucretia."

"Oh, go dance up a rope," she said, surprising Quincannon if not her husband.

Meeker performed his puffing-toad imitation and started to say something, but at that moment the door burst open and the wind blew in a young man swathed in a greatcoat, scarf, gloves, and stocking cap. His lean, clean-shaven face—weak-chinned and thin-lipped—was ruddy from the cold. Jared Meeker, in the flesh.

His parents might have been two sticks of furniture for all he had to say to them. It wasn't until he opened his coat and yanked off his cap, revealing a mop of ginger-colored hair, that he noticed Quincannon. "Well, a visitor. And a stranger at that."

"His name is John Quincannon," Mrs. Meeker said. "He's a detective."

The last word caused Jared's eyes to narrow. "A detective? What kind of detective? What's he doing here?"

"Your father hired him to investigate the supernatural. Of all things."

". . . Ah. The ghost, you mean?"

"Whatever it is we've seen these past two nights, yes," Meeker said.

Jared relaxed into an indolent posture as he shed his coat. Then he laughed, a thin barking sound like that of an adenoidal seal. "A detective to investigate a ghost. *Hah!* That's rich, that is."

Quincannon said: "I have had stranger cases, and brought them to a satisfactory conclusion. Are you a believer or a skeptic, lad?"

"I believe what I see with my own eyes. What about you?"

"I have an open mind on the subject," he lied.

"Well, it's a real ghost, all right. Likely of a man who died in one of the cars, or in a railway accident. Couldn't be anything else, no matter what anybody thinks. You may well see it for yourself, if you're planning to spend the night."

"I am."

"If it does reappear, you'll be a believer, too."

"We'll see about that."

Jared grinned and loosed another bark. "A detective. *Hah!*"

Alone in the parlor, Quincannon smoked his stubby briar and waited for the hands on his stem-winder to point to 11:30 p.m. The Meekers had all retired to their respective bedrooms in the end cars some time earlier, at his insistence; he preferred to maintain a solitary vigil. He also preferred silence to desultory and pointless conversation. There were ominous rumblings in his digestive tract as well, the result of the bland chicken dish and boiled potatoes and carrots Mrs. Meeker had seen fit to serve for supper.

The car was no longer overheated, now that the fire in the stove had banked. Cooling, the stove metal made little *pinging* sounds that punctuated the *snicking* of wind-flung sand against the car's windows and sides. As 11:30 p.m. approached, he checked the loads in his Navy Colt. Not that he expected to need the weapon—the Carville ghost seemed to have no malevolent intention, and no one had ever succeeded in plugging a spook in any case—but he had learned long ago to exercise caution in all situations.

It was time. He holstered the Navy, donned his greatcoat, cap, scarf, and gloves, and slipped out into the night.

Icy, fog-wet wind and blowing sand buffeted him as he came down off the walkway. The night was not quite black as tar but close to it; he could barely make out the shed and corral nearby. The distant jumble of abandoned cars was invisible except for brief rents in the wall of fog, and then discernible only as faintly lumpish shapes among the dunes.

He slogged into the shelter of the lean-to. The two horses, both blanketed against the cold, stirred and one nickered softly at his passage. He removed his dark lantern from beneath the seat of the rented buggy, lighted it, closed the shutter, and then went to the side wall and probed along it until he found a gap between boards. Another brief tear in the fog permitted him to fix the proper angle for viewing the cars. He dragged over two bales of hay, piled one atop the other, and perched on the makeshift seat. By bending forward slightly, his eyes were on a level with the gap. He settled down to wait.

He had learned patience in situations such as this, by ruminating on matters of business and pleasure. Sabina occupied his mind for a considerable time. Then he sighed and shifted his thoughts to the other cases currently under investigation. The missing Devereaux heiress should be easy enough to locate; like as not she had gone off for an extended dalliance with one of her swains, since no ransom demand had been received by the family. Sabina needed no help from him in yaffling the pickpocket at the Chutes amusement park. The Wells Fargo robbery was more his type of case, and a challenging one since city bluecoats and rival detective agencies were also on the hunt for the two masked bandits who had escaped with $25,000 in cash. He had to admit that he'd made little enough headway over the past two weeks, but the same was true of his competitors for the reward Wells Fargo was offering.

Light. A faint shimmery glow through the mist.

He strained forward, squinting closer to the gap. Gray-black for a few seconds, then the fog lifted somewhat and he spied the eerie radiance again, shifting about behind the windows in one of the cars. More than just a glow—an ectoplasmic shape, an unearthly face.

He snatched up the dark lantern, hopped off the hay bales, and stepped out around the corner of the lean-to. The thing continued to drift around inside the car, held stationary for a few seconds, moved again. Quincannon was moving himself by then, over into the shadow of the cistern. Beyond there, flattish sand fields stretched for thirty or forty rods on three sides; there was no cover anywhere on its expanse, no quick way to get to the cars, even by circling around, without crossing open space.

He waited for a thickening of the fog, then stepped out in a low crouch and ran toward the car. He was halfway there when the radiance vanished.

Immediately he veered to his right, toward the line of dunes behind the cars. But he couldn't generate any speed; in the wet darkness and loose sand he felt as if he were churning, heavy-legged, through a dream. There were no sounds except for the wind, the distant pound of surf, the rasp of his breathing.

It was two or three minutes before he reached the foot of the nearest dune. No sooner had he begun to plow upward along its steep side than the wraith-like human shape appeared suddenly at the crest and then bounded away in a rush of shimmery phosphorescence.

Quincannon shined the lantern in that direction, but the beam wasn't powerful enough to cut through the wall of fog. Cursing, he leaned forward and dug his free hand into the sand to help propel himself upward. Behind and below him, he heard a shout. A quick glance over his shoulder told him it had come from a man running across the sand field—Barnaby or Jared Meeker, alerted too late to be of any assistance.

He was a few feet from the crest when a wind-muffled report reached his ears. The ghost shape twitched, seemed to bound forward another step or two, and then suddenly vanished. Two or three heartbeats later, it reappeared, higher up, twisted, and was gone again.

Quincannon filled his right hand with his Navy Colt as he struggled, panting, to the dune top. When he straightened, he thought he saw another flash of radiance in the far distance. After that, there was nothing to see but fog and darkness.

He made his way forward, playing the lantern beam ahead of him. The grassy surface of this dune and the next in line showed no marks of passage. But down near the bottom on the opposite side, the light illuminated a faint, irregular line of tracks that the wind was already beginning to erase.

It illuminated something else below as he climbed atop the third dune—the dark figure of a man sprawled face down in the sand.

Panting sounds reached his ears; a few moments later, Barnaby Meeker hove into view and staggered toward him. Quincannon didn't wait. He half slid down the sandhill to the motionless figure at the bottom, anchored the lantern so that the beam shone fully on the dark-clothed man, and turned him over. The staring eyes conveyed that he was beyond help. The gaping wound on his chest stated he'd been shot.

Meeker came sliding down the hill, pulled up, and emitted a cry of anguish. "Jared! Oh, my God, it's Jared!"

Quincannon cast his gaze back along the dunes. The line of irregular footprints led straight to where Jared Meeker lay. There were no others in the vicinity except for those made by Quincannon and Barnaby Meeker.

At dawn Quincannon helped his distraught employer hitch up his wagon. There were no telephones in Carville; Meeker would have to drive to the nearest one to summon the city police and coroner. Young Jared's body had been carried to his bedroom car, and Mrs. Meeker had held a vigil there most of the night. Despite her disparaging comments about her son, she had been inconsolable when she learned of his death. And she'd made no bones about blaming Quincannon for what had happened, screaming at him: "What kind of detective are you, allowing my poor boy to be murdered right before your eyes?"

For his part, Quincannon was in a dark humor. As unjust as Mrs. Meeker's tirade had been, Jared Meeker *had* been murdered more or less before his eyes. He couldn't have foreseen what would happen, of course, but the shooting was a potential blow to his reputation. If he failed to find out who was responsible, and why, the confounded newspapers would have a field day at his expense.

One thing was certain, and the apparent evidence to the contrary be damned: Jared Meeker had not been mortally wounded by a malevolent spirit from the Other Side. Spooks do not carry guns, nor can ectoplasm aim and fire one with deadly accuracy in foggy darkness.

When Meeker had gone on his way, Quincannon embarked on his first order of business—a talk with Artemus Crabb. Crabb had failed to put in an appearance at any time during last night's bizarre happenings, which may or may not have an innocent explanation. The fog was still present this morning, but the wind had died down and visibility was good. The dunes lay like a desert wasteland all around him as he trudged down the left fork to Crabb's car.

Knuckles on the rough-hewn door produced no response, neither did a brace of shouts. Not home at this hour? Quincannon used his fist on the door, and raised his call of Crabb's name to a tolerable bellow. This produced results. Crabb was home, and had apparently been asleep. He jerked the door open, wearing a pair of loose-fitting long johns, and glared at Quincannon out of sleep-puffed eyes.

"You," he said. "What the devil's the idea, waking me up this early?"

Quincannon said bluntly: "One of your neighbors was murdered last night."

"What? What's that? Who was murdered?"

"Jared Meeker. From all appearances, he was done in by the Carville ghost."

Crabb recoiled a step, his eyes popping wide. "The hell you say. The . . . ghost? Last night?"

"On the prowl again, the same as before. You didn't see it?"

"Not me. Once was enough. I don't want nothing to do with spooks. I bolted my door, shuttered all the windows, and went to bed with a weapon close to hand."

"Heard nothing, either, I take it?"

"Just the wind. Where'd it happen?"

"On the dunes beyond the abandoned cars."

"I don't get it," Crabb said. "How can a damned ghost shoot a man?"

"A ghost can't. A man did."

"What man? Who'd want to kill the Meeker kid?"

Quincannon smiled wolfishly. "Who, indeed?"

He left Crabb in the doorway and made his way past the jumble of abandoned cars, around behind the line of dunes where he'd last seen the white radiance. A careful search of the wind-smoothed sand along their backsides turned up nothing. Opposite where he had found Jared Meeker was another high-topped dune; he climbed it and inspected the sparse vegetation that grew along the crest.

Ah, just as he'd suspected. Some of the grass stalks had broken ends and a patch of gorse was gouged and mashed flat. This was where the assassin had lain to fire the fatal shot—and a marksman he was, to have been so accurate on a night like the last.

Quincannon searched behind the dune. Here and there, in places sheltered from the wind, were footprints leading to and from the abandoned cars. Then he began to range outward in the opposite direction, zigzagging back and forth among the sandhills. Gulls wheeled overhead, shrieking, as he drew nearer to the beach. The Pacific was calmer this morning, the waves breaking more quietly over the white sand.

For more than an hour he continued his hunt. He found nothing among the dunes. The long inner sweep of the beach was littered with all manner of flotsam cast up during storms and high winds— shells, bottles, tins, driftwood large and small, birds and sea creatures alive and dead. Last night's wind had been blowing from the southeast; he ranged farther to the north, his sharp eyes scanning left and right.

Some 200 rods from where he had emerged onto the beach, he found what he was looking for. Or rather, the wreckage of what he was looking for, caught and tangled around the bare limb of a tree branch.

He extricated it carefully, examined it, and tucked it inside his coat. After which, whistling a temperance tune off key, he retraced his path along the beach, through the dunes, and back to the Meekers' home.

The car that had been Jared Meeker's bedroom was the northernmost of the four. The curtains had been drawn over the windows; he went to the door, knocked discreetly, received no response. Mrs. Meeker, as he'd hoped, had given up her vigil and gone to one of the other cars. He tried the latch, found it unlocked, stepped inside, and shut the door behind him.

The dead man lay on his bed, covered by a blanket provided by his mother. The rest of the room contained a stove, a few pieces of mismatched furniture, a steamer trunk, a framed Wild West show poster depicting a cowboy riding a wildly bucking bronco, and little else. Quincannon searched the dresser drawers first, then the steamer trunk. Several items of interest were tucked inside the latter—hand tools, a ball of twine, a jar of oil-based paint, a board with four ten-penny nails driven through it, and two lead sinkers that matched in size and shape the one he'd found yesterday in the abandoned car.

He left the items where they lay and was closing the trunk's lid when the door opened and Mrs.

Meeker entered. She emitted a startled gasp when she saw him. "Mister Quincannon! How dare you come in here without permission?"

"My apologies. But it was necessary."

"Necessary? Prowling through my dead son's possessions?"

"To the conclusion of my investigation."

". . . Are you saying you know who murdered Jared?"

Before he could respond, a hailing shout came from outside. Barnaby Meeker had returned. And not alone. With him were the city coroner in a morgue wagon, and a plainclothes homicide detective named Hiram Dooley in a police hack driven by a bluecoat.

Dooley was middle-aged, portly, sported a thick brushy mustache, and had a complexion the exact hue of cooked beets. Stretched across his bulging middle was a gold watch chain adorned with an elk's tooth the size of a golf ball. His first words to Quincannon were: "I've heard of you, laddybuck. You and that female partner of yours."

"Only in the most glowing terms, no doubt."

"*Hah.* Just because you've counted yourselves lucky on a few cases doesn't mark you high in my book. I don't like fly cops."

And I don't like pompous, empty-headed civil servants, Quincannon thought, but he only smiled and said: "Perhaps I'll count myself lucky, as you put it, on this case as well."

"Yeah? We'll see about that."

That we will, Inspector. And sooner than you think.

Meeker had already given Dooley an account of last night's events, but the homicide dick demanded another from Quincannon. He scoffed at what he called "this spook hokum" and seemed skeptical, if not openly suspicious, of Quincannon's rôle in the matter. Quincannon bore his browbeating with good-natured equanimity. He could have told Dooley then and there what he had deduced, but the man's manner irritated him and he took a certain amount of pleasure in watching him blunder and bluster about Jared's bedroom and the scene of the murder, overlooking clues and asking the wrong questions. While the two policemen were examining the abandoned cars, Quincannon took Barnaby Meeker aside and asked him a pair of seemingly innocuous questions. The answers he received were the ones he had expected.

As Dooley and the bluecoat emerged, Artemus Crabb came striding over from the direction of his car. Crabb seemed more at ease this time, his face reflecting curiosity rather than hostility or concern. He barely glanced at Quincannon, his attention focused on the law dogs.

"And who would you be?" Dooley demanded.

"Crabb's my name. I live over yonder."

Dooley introduced himself. "I been told you

didn't see anything of what happened out here last night."

"That's right, I didn't. Seen the spook lights the night before and once is enough for me. I spent last night locked up inside my car."

"No, you didn't," Quincannon said.

"What's that?"

"You spent part of the night lying in wait on one of the dunes, with a cocked revolver in your hand."

"What the devil would I do that for?"

"To lay the Carville ghost, once and for all."

All eyes were on Quincannon now, Crabb glaring with feigned indignation, Dooley and Meeker showing their surprise. Quincannon favored them with the smile he reserved for moments such as these. It was time for him to take center stage, to reveal the deductive prowess that made him, in his estimation, the finest detective west of the Mississippi—a rôle he relished above all others.

Meeker said: "What are you saying, Mister Quincannon? That Crabb murdered my son?"

"With malice aforethought."

"That's a damn' lie!" Crabb snapped. "Spook stuff scares the bejesus out of me. Ask Meeker, ask that old coot in the coffee saloon . . . they'll tell you."

"Spook stuff that you fear might be authentic, yes. But by the time you crouched in wait last night, you knew the truth about the Carville ghost."

"What truth?" Dooley demanded.

"That it was all a sham designed to separate Mister Crabb from his cache of loot."

"Loot? What loot?"

"The twenty-five thousand dollars he and his accomplice stole from Wells Fargo Express two weeks ago."

Dooley gawped at him. Crabb shouted: "You're crazy! You can't pin that on me. You can't prove anything against me."

"I can prove that you murdered Jared Meeker," Quincannon said, "by your own testimony. When I told you this morning that he'd been killed, you said . . . 'How can a damned ghost shoot a man?' But I didn't say how he'd been killed. How did you know he'd been shot unless you pulled the trigger yourself?"

"I just . . . ah . . . assumed it. . . ."

"Bosh. You had no reason to assume such a fact." Quincannon turned his attention to Dooley. "Jared Meeker was shot with a large-bore handgun, one with a considerable range . . . the very type Crabb carries. A search of his premises should provide additional evidence. Though not the loot from the robbery, or else Jared would have found it. It's hidden elsewhere, likely buried under or near one of those abandoned cars. . . ."

"Hold on, Quincannon," Dooley said. "You telling us Jared Meeker knew Crabb was one of the bandits?"

"He did . . . because he was the other one, Crabb's accomplice."

Meeker emitted a wounded sound, puffed up, and stabbed the sand with his blackthorn stick. "That can't be true!"

"But I'm afraid it is," Quincannon said. "You told me yourself just now that the only job Jared held in his young life was that of a clerk in a shoe emporium on Kearney Street downtown . . . the same street and the very same block on which the Wells Fargo Express office is located, and a perfect position to observe the days and times large sums of cash were delivered. He fell in somehow with Crabb and together they planned and executed the robbery. Afterward they separated, Crabb evidently keeping the loot with him. The plan then called for Crabb to take up residence here in Carville, a place known to have been used before as a temporary hide-out by criminals, until the hunt for the stolen money grew cold.

"My guess is that Jared grew impatient for his share of the spoils and Crabb refused to give it to him or to reveal where he'd hidden it. His first action would have been to search Crabb's car when Crabb was away on one of his infrequent outings. When he didn't find the loot, he embarked on a more devious, and foolish, course."

Dooley asked: "Why didn't he just throw down on Crabb and demand his share?"

"The lad wasn't made that way. He was a sly schemer and likely something of a coward, afraid of a direct confrontation with his partner in crime. I'm sorry, Mister Meeker, but the evidence supports this conclusion."

Meeker said nothing. He appeared to be slowly deflating.

Quincannon went on: "At some point during their relationship, Crabb revealed to Jared his fear of the supernatural. This was the core of the lad's too-clever plan. He would frighten Crabb enough to force him to leave Carville after first digging up and dividing the loot. But he was careless enough to say or do something to alert Crabb to the game he was playing. That, and the probable fact that Crabb wanted the entire booty for himself, cost Jared his life."

"So he was responsible for the spook business," Dooley said.

"More than just responsible. He was the Carville ghost."

"And just how did he manage that?"

"A remark Missus Meeker made yesterday alerted me to the method. She said that he was 'a kiting youngster.' At the time I took that to mean flighty, the runabout sort, but she meant it literally. His passion as a boy, as Mister Meeker confirmed to me a few minutes ago, was flying kites."

"What does that have to do with . . . ?"

Dooley stopped speaking abruptly. For just then Quincannon had removed from beneath his coat the wreckage he'd found earlier on the beach

"This is the Carville ghost, or what's left of it," he said. "A simple kite made of heavy canvas tacked onto a wooden frame, roughly fashioned in the shape of a man and coated with an oil-based paint mixed with phosphorous . . . all the tools for the making of which you'll find in Jared's steamer trunk. His game went like this. First he told Crabb that he'd seen spook lights among the abandoned cars and to watch for them himself. Then, past midnight, he slipped out, went to one of the cars, flashed the kite about to create the illusion of an otherworldly glow, used a tool made of a piece of wood and several nails . . . which you'll also find in his trunk . . . to make claw-like scratches on the walls and floors, and then fled with the kite before Crabb or anyone else could catch him."

Meeker asked dully: "How could he run across the tops of the dunes without leaving tracks?"

"He didn't run across the tops, he ran along below and behind the dunes with the string played out just far enough to lift the kite above the crests. To hold it at that height, he used these"— Quincannon held out one of the lead sinkers he'd found—"to weight it down so he could control it in the wind. On dark, foggy nights, seen from a distance and manipulated by an expert kite flier, the kite gave every appearance of a ghostly figure bounding across the sandhills. And when he wanted it to disappear, he merely yanked it down out of sight, drew it in, and hid it under his coat. That was what he was about to do when Crabb shot him. When the bullet struck him, the string loosed from his hand and the kite was carried off by the wind. I saw flashes of phosphorescence, higher up, before it disappeared altogether. This morning I found the remains on the beach."

Dooley said grudgingly: "By Godfrey, it all makes sense. You, Crabb, what do you have to say for yourself now?"

"Just this." And before anyone could move, Crabb's hand snaked under his coat and came out holding the large-bore Bisley Colt. "I didn't let that featherbrain kid get his hands on this money and I ain't about to let you do it, either. The lot of you, move on over to that car of mine."

Nobody moved except Crabb. He backed up a step. "I mean it," he said. "Be locked up until I'm clear or take a bullet where you stand. One killing or several, it don't make any difference to me."

He backed up another step. Unfortunately for him, the direction he took brought him just close enough for Quincannon to swat him with the wrecked kite. The blow pitched him off balance;

before he could bring his weapon to bear again, Quincannon thumped him once on the temple and once on the point of the jaw. Crabb obligingly dropped the revolver and lay down quietly in the sand.

Quincannon massaged his bruised knuckles. "And what do you think of fly cops now, laddybuck?" he asked Dooley. "Do you mark John Quincannon higher in that book of yours than before?"

Dooley, bending down to Crabb with a pair of handcuffs, muttered something that Quincannon—perhaps fortunately—failed to catch.

Artemus Crabb, with a certain amount of persuasion from Dooley and the bluecoat, confessed to the robbery and the murder of Jared Meeker—the details of both being for the most part as Quincannon had surmised. The Wells Fargo money turned out to be buried beneath one of the abandoned cars; the full amount was there, not a penny having been spent.

Crabb and the loot were carted away in the police hack, and young Jared's remains in the morgue wagon. The Meekers followed the coroner in their buggy. Neither had anything to say to Quincannon, although Mrs. Meeker fixed him with a baleful glare as they pulled out. He supposed that the $1,000 Barnaby Meeker had promised him would not be paid, but even if it was offered, he would be hard pressed to accept it under the circumstances. He felt sympathy for the Meekers. The loss of a wastrel son was no less painful than the loss of a saintly one.

Besides, he thought as he clattered the rented buggy after the others, he would be well recompensed for his twenty-four hours in Carville-by-the-Sea and his usual brilliant detective work. The reward offered by Wells Fargo for the return of the stolen funds was ten percent of the total—the not inconsiderable sum of $2,500 to fatten the coffers of Carpenter and Quincannon, Professional Detective Services.

A smile creased his whiskers. A reward of that magnitude might well induce Sabina to change her mind about having dinner with him at Marchand's French Restaurant. It might even induce her to change her mind about another type of celebratory entertainment. Women were mutable creatures, after all, and John Quincannon was nothing if not persistent. One of these evenings he might yet be gifted with the only reward he coveted more than the purely financial. . . .

PICKPOCKET

A Sabina Carpenter Story

by Marcia Muller

Sabina Carpenter put on her straw picture hat and contemplated the hatpins in the velvet cushion on her bureau. After a moment she selected a Charles Horner design of silver and coral and skewered the hat to her upswept dark hair. The hatpin, a gift on her last birthday, was one of two she owned by the famed British designer. The other, a butterfly with an onyx body and diamond-chip wings was a gift from her late husband and much too ornate—to say nothing of valuable—to wear during the day.

Momentarily she recalled Stephen's face: thin, with prominent cheek bones and chin. Brilliant blue eyes below dark brown hair. A face that could radiate tenderness—and danger. Like herself, a Pinkerton detective in Denver, he had been working on a land-fraud case when he was shot to death in a raid. It troubled Sabina that over the past few years his features had become less distinct in her memory, as had those of her deceased parents, but she assumed that was human nature. One's memories blur; one goes on.

She scrutinized her reflection in the mirror and concluded that she looked more like a respectable young matron than a private detective setting out to trap a pickpocket. Satisfied, she left her second-story Russian Hill flat, passed through the iron picket fence, and entered a hansom cab that she had earlier engaged. It took her down Van Ness Avenue and south on Haight Street.

The journey was a lengthy one, passing through sparsely settled areas of the city, and it gave Sabina time to reflect upon the job ahead. Charles Ackerman, owner of the Haight Street Chutes amusement park and an attorney for the Southern Pacific and the Market Street and Sutter Street Railroads, had come to the offices of Carpenter and Quincannon, Professional Detective Services, the previous morning. Sabina's partner, John Quincannon, had been out of sorts because she had just refused his invitation to dinner at Marchand's French restaurant. Sabina, a practical woman, refused many of John's frequent invitations. Mixing business with pleasure was a dangerous proposition; it could imperil their partnership, an arrangement she was very happy with as it stood. . . .

And yet, she did not find John unattractive. Quite the opposite. . . .

Sternly Sabina turned her thoughts to the business at hand. Charles Ackerman had a problem at his newly opened amusement park on Haight Street near the southern edge of Golden Gate Park. Patrons had complained that a pickpocket was operating in the park, yet neither his employees nor the police had yet to observe any of the more notorious dips and cutpurses who worked the San Francisco streets. A clever woman, Ackerman said with a nod at Sabina, might be able to succeed where they had failed. John bristled at being excluded, then lapsed into a grumpy silence. Sabina and Ackerman concluded the conversation and agreed she would come to the park the next morning, after she had finished with another bit of pressing business.

The hack pulled to the curb between Cole and Clayton Streets. Sabina paid the driver and alighted, then turned toward the park. Its most prominent feature was a 300-foot long Shoot-the-Chutes, a double trestled track that rose seventy feet into the air. Passengers would ascend to a room at the top of the slides, where they would board boats for a swift descent to an artificial lake at the bottom. Sabina had heard that the ride was quite thrilling—or frightening, according to the person's perspective. She herself would enjoy trying it.

In addition to the water slide, the park contained a scenic railway, a merry-go-round, various carnival-like establishments, and a refreshment stand. Ackerman had told Sabina she would find his manager, Lester Sweeney, in the office beyond the ticket booth. She crossed the street, holding up her slim flowered skirt so the hem wouldn't get dusty, and asked at the booth for Mr. Sweeney. The man collecting admissions motioned her inside and through a door behind him.

Sweeney was at a desk that seemed too large for the cramped space, adding a column of figures. He was a big man, possibly in his late forties, with thinning red hair and a complexion that spoke of a fondness for strong drink. When he looked up at Sabina, his eyes, reddened and surrounded by pouched flesh, gleamed in appreciation. Quickly she presented her card, and the gleam faded.

"Please sit down, Missus Carpenter," he said. "Mister Ackerman told me you'd be coming this morning."

"Thank you." Sabina sat on the single wooden chair sandwiched between the desk and the wall. "What can you tell me about these pickpocketing incidents?"

"They have occurred over the past two weeks, at different times of day. Eight in all. Word is spreading, and we're bound to lose customers."

"You spoke with the victims?"

"Yes, and there may have been others who didn't report the incidents."

"Was there anything in common that was reported?"

Sweeney frowned, thinking. The frown had an alarming effect on his face, making it look like something that had softened and spread after being left out in the rain. In a moment he shook his head. "Nothing that I can recall."

"Do you have the victims' names and addresses?"

"Somewhere here." He began to shuffle through the many papers on his desk.

Sabina held up a hand and stood. "I'll return to collect the list later. In the meantime, I trust I may have full access to the park?"

"Certainly, Missus Carpenter."

Several hours later Sabina, who was familiar with most of San Francisco's dips and cutpurses, had ascertained that none of them was working the Chutes. Notably absent were Fanny Spigott, dubbed "Queen of the Pickpockets," and her husband Joe, "King of the Pickpockets," who recently had plotted—unsuccessfully—to steal the 2,000-pound statue of Venus de Milo from the Louvre Museum in Paris. Also among the absent were Lil Hamlin, "Fainting Lil," whose ploy was to pass out in the arms of her victims; Jane O'Leary, "Weeping Jane," who lured her marks in by enlisting them in the hunt for her missing six-year-old, then relieved them of their valuables while hugging them when the precocious and well-trained child was found; "Fingers" McCoy claimed to have the fastest reach in town, and "Lovely Lena," true name unknown, a blonde so captivating that it was said she blinded her victims.

While searching for her pickpocket, Sabina had toured the park on the scenic railway, eaten an ice cream, ridden the merry-go-round, and taken a boatride down the Chutes—which was indeed thrilling. So thrilling that she rewarded her bravery with a German sausage on a sourdough roll. It was early afternoon and she was leaving Lester Sweeney's office with the list of the pickpocket's victims when she saw an unaccompanied woman intensely watching the crowd around the merry-go-round. The woman moved foward, next to a man in a straw bowler, but when he turned and nodded to her, she stepped a few paces away.

Sabina moved closer.

The woman had light brown hair, upswept under a wide-brimmed straw picture hat similar to Sabina's. She was slender, outfitted in a white shirtwaist and cornflower blue skirt. The hat shaded her features, and the only distinctive thing about her attire was the pin that held the hat to her head. Sabina—a connoisseur of hatpins—recognized it as a Charles Horner of blue glass overlaid with a gold pattern.

The woman must have felt Sabina's gaze. She looked around, and Sabina saw she had blue eyes and rather plain features, except for a small white scar on her chin. Her gaze slid over Sabina, focused on a man to her right, but moved away when he reached down to pick up a fretting child, After a moment the woman turned and walked slowly toward the exit.

A pickpocket, for certain; Sabina had seen how

they operated many times. She followed, keeping her eyes on the distinctive hatpin.

Fortunately there was a row of hansom cabs waiting outside the gates of the park. The woman with the distinctive hatpin claimed the first of these, and Sabina took another, asking the driver to follow the other hack. He regarded her curiously, no doubt unused to gentlewomen making such requests, but the new century was rapidly approaching, and with it what the press had dubbed the New Woman. Very often these days the female sex did not think or act as it once had.

The brown-haired woman's cab led them north on Haight and finally to Market Street, the city's main artery. There she disembarked near the Palace Hotel—as did Sabina—and crossed Market to Montgomery. It was 5:00 p.m. and businessmen of all kinds were pouring out of their downtown offices to travel the Cocktail Route, as the Gay Nineties young blades termed it.

From the Reception Saloon on Sutter Street to Haquette's Palace of Art on Post Street to the Palace Hotel Bar, the influential men of San Francisco trekked daily, partaking of fine liquor and lavish free banquet spreads. Women—at least respectable ones—were not admitted to these establishments, but Sabina had ample knowledge of them from John's tales of the days when he was a drinking man. He had been an operative with the

U.S. Secret Service, until the accidental death by his hand of a pregnant woman turned him into a drunkard; those were the days before he met Sabina and embarked on a new, sober life. . . .

Once again she forced her thoughts away from John Quincannon.

The woman she had followed from the amusement park was now well into the crowd on Montgomery Street—known as The Ambrosial Path to cocktail hour revelers. Street characters and vendors, beggars and ad-carriers for the various saloons' free lunches, temperance speakers, and the Salvation Army band—all mingled with well-dressed bankers and attorneys, politicians and physicians. Sabina made her way through the throng, keeping her eye on the woman's hat, brushing aside the importunings of a match-peddler. The woman moved along unhurriedly and after two blocks turned left and walked over to Kearney.

There the street scene was even livelier: palm readers, shooting galleries, and auction houses had their quarters there. Ever present were the shouting vendors and pitchmen of all sorts; fakirs and touters of Marxism; snake charmers and speech makers of all persuasions. It seemed every type of individual in the world had come to Kearney Street for the start of the evening. Sabina kept her eyes on the woman as she moved at a leisurely pace, stopping to finger a bolt of Indian fabric and then to listen to a speaker extol the virtues of phrenology. She moved deeper into the crowd, and Sabina momentarily lost her; seconds later she heard a faint cry and pushed her way forward.

A gent in a frock coat was bent over, his silk hat having fallen to the sidewalk. As he straightened, his face frozen in a grimace of pain, he reached inside his coat. Sudden anger replaced pain and he shouted: "Stop, thief!"

But no one was fleeing. The crowd murmured, heads swiveling, faces curious and alarmed. The man again shouted: "My watch! I've been robbed!"

Sabina moved forward. "What happened?"

The man stared at her, open-mouthed.

She hurriedly removed one of her cards from her reticule and gave it to him. "I am investigating a series of thefts. Please tell me what happened."

He examined the card. "Will you find the person who took my watch? It is very old and rare. . . ."

"Was it you who cried out earlier?"

"Yes. I suffered a sharp pain in my side. Here." He indicated his lower left ribcage. "I have had such discomfort before, and I've just come from the Bank Exchange where, I'm afraid, I consumed an overlarge quantity of oysters on the half shell. I suppose the thief took advantage of my distress."

"Did you not notice anyone close to you? A woman, perhaps?"

The gent shook his head. "I saw no one."

Sabina turned to the ring of people surrounding them, asked the same question of them, and received the same answer.

The woman she'd followed from the amusement park had found her mark, struck, and swiftly vanished.

It was nearly 7:00 p.m., an inconvenient time to go calling, but over the course of her years as a Pinkerton operative and a self-employed detective, Sabina had become accustomed to calling on people at inconvenient times.

At her flat on Russian Hill, she changed into a heavy black skirt and shirtwaist and a long cape in deference to the foggy San Francisco evening. Once again she left in a hansom cab, one she'd hired to wait for her at her stops along the way. She had studied the list of names of the pickpocket's victims that Lester Sweeney had given her, and mapped out a convenient and easy route.

Her first destination was the home of Mr. William Buchanan on Green Street near Van Ness Avenue. Mr. Buchanan was not at home, the maid who answered the door told her. He and Mrs. Buchanan had gone to their country house on the Peninsula for two weeks.

In the cab again, Sabina crossed Mr. Buchanan's name off the list, and instructed the driver to take her to an address on Webster Street in the Western Addition.

The house there was large and elegant, and Mr. John Greenway resembled many of the well-attired gentlemen Sabina had earlier seen parading on the Cocktail Route. He greeted her cordially, taking her into the front parlor and introducing her to his attractive wife, who looked to be expecting a child.

"A note from Mister Sweeney at the Chutes was delivered this afternoon," he told Sabina. "It said you wish to speak with me concerning the theft of my diamond stickpin. I hope I can help you."

"As do I. What were the circumstances of the theft?"

Greenway glanced at his auburn-haired wife, who smiled encouragingly. "We had ridden the water slide and stopped at the refreshment stand for a glass of lemonade," he said. "The ride had made me feel unwell, so we decided to come home. There was a large crowd watching a juggler near the gates, and we were separated in it. I felt a sharp pain in my side . . . the result of the ride, I suppose . . . and momentarily became disoriented. When I recovered, and my wife rejoined me, she saw that my stickpin was missing."

Men in distress, Sabina thought. *A clever pickpocket noting this and taking advantage of their momentary confusion.*

She thanked the Greenways and took her leave.

No one came to the door at either of the next two victims' residences, but at a small Eastlake-style Victorian near Lafayette Square, Sabina was greeted by the plump young daughter of Mr. George Anderson. Her parents, the daughter said, were at the Orpheum, a vaudeville house on O'Farrell Street. Could she reveal anything about the distressing incident at the amusement park? Sabina asked. Certainly, the daughter said, she had witnessed it.

In the small front parlor, Ellen Anderson rang for the housekeeper and ordered tea. It came quickly, accompanied by a plate of ginger cookies. Sabina took one as Miss Anderson poured and prattled on about her excitement about meeting a lady detective. Then she proceeded with her questioning.

"You were with your father at the amusement park when his purse was stolen?"

"My mother, my brother, and I."

"Tell me what you saw, please."

"We were near the merry-go-round. It was very crowded, children waiting to board and parents watching their children on the ride. Allen, my brother, was trying to persuade me to ride with him. He's only ten years old, so a merry-go-round is a thrill for him, but I'm sixteen, and it seems so very childish. . . ."

"Did you ride anyway?"

"No. But Allen did. We were watching him when suddenly my father groaned. He took hold of his side, slued around, and staggered a few paces. Mother and I caught him before he could fall. When we'd righted him, he found all his money was gone."

"What caused this sudden pain?"

"A gastric distress, apparently."

"Does your father normally suffer from digestive problems?"

"No, but earlier we'd had hot sausages at the refreshment stand. We assumed they were what affected him and then a thief had taken advantage of the moment."

Every thief has his or her own method, Sabina thought, *and evidently this one's was to seek out people who had fallen ill and were therefore vulnerable.*

"Did your father talk about the incident afterwards?"

Ellen Anderson shook her dark-curled head. "He seemed ashamed of being robbed. In fact, Mother had to insist he report the theft to the park manager."

"Did his distress continue afterwards?"

"I don't think so, but he's never been one to talk about his ailments."

Two more fruitless stops left her with a final name on the list: Henry Holbrooke, on South Park. The oval-shaped park, an exact copy of London's Berkeley Square, had once been home to the reigning society of San Francisco, but now its grandeur, and that of neighboring Rincon Hill, was fading. Most of the powerful millionaires and their families who had resided there had moved to more fashionable venues such as Nob Hill, and many of the elegant homes looked somewhat shopworn. Henry Holbrooke's was one of the latter, its paint peeling and small front garden unkempt, a grand old lady slipping into genteel poverty.

A light was burning behind heavy velvet curtains in a bay window, but when Sabina knocked, no one answered. She knocked again, and after a moment the door opened. The inner hallway was so dark that she could scarcely make out the person standing there. Then she saw it was a woman dressed entirely in black. She said: "Missus Holbrooke?"

"Yes." The woman's voice cracked, as if rusty from disuse.

Sabina gave her name and explained her mission. The woman made no move to take the card she extended.

"May I speak with your husband?" Sabina asked.

"My husband is dead."

". . . My condolences. May I ask when he passed on?"

"Two weeks ago."

That would have been a week after he was robbed of his money belt at the Chutes.

"May I come in?" Sabina asked.

"I'd rather you didn't. I've been . . . tearful. I don't wish for anyone to see me after I've been weeping."

"I understand. What was the cause of your husband's death?"

"An infection and internal bleeding."

"Had he been ill long?"

"He had never been ill. Not a day in his life."

"What did his physician say?"

The widow laughed harshly. "We couldn't afford a physician, not after his money belt was stolen. He died at home, in my arms, and the coroner came and took him away. I had to sell my jewelry . . . what was left of it . . . so he could have a decent burial."

"I'm sorry. Why did he have so much money on his person during an afternoon at the amusement park?"

"My husband never went anywhere without that belt. He was afraid to leave it at home. This neighborhood is not what it once was."

Sabina glanced at the neighboring homes in their fading glory. Henry Holbrooke would have been better advised to keep his money in a bank.

"Did the coroner tell you what might have caused your husband's infection?" she asked.

Mrs. Holbrooke leaned heavily on the doorjamb; like South Park, she was slowly deteriorating. "No. Only that it resulted in internal bleeding." The woman reached out and placed a hand on Sabina's arm. "If you apprehend the thief, will you recover my husband's money?"

Most likely it had already been spent, but Sabina said: "Perhaps."

"Will you return it to me? I'd like to buy him a good grave marker."

"Of course."

If the money had indeed been spent, Sabina resolved that Carpenter and Quincannon would supply the grave marker, out of the handsome fee Charles Ackerman would pay them—whether John liked it or not.

Sabina returned to the hansom, but asked the driver to wait. A pickpocket, she thought, rarely works the same territory in a single day. The woman she had followed was unlikely to return to the Chutes in the near future; she'd seen Sabina eyeing her suspiciously. The Ambrosial Path would be similarly off limits, since she'd had success there and word would by now have spread among the habitués of the area. Where else would a pickpocket who preyed on the infirm go to ply her trade?

After a moment, Sabina said to the hack driver: "Take me to Market and Fourth Streets, please."

• • •

The open field at Market and Fourth was brightly lit by lanterns and torchlights, and dotted with tents and wagons. Music filled the air from many sources, each competing with the other; barkers shouted, and a group of Negro minstrels sang "Swing Low, Sweet Chariot." Sabina stood at the field's perimeter, surveying the medicine show.

From the wagons men hawked well-known remedies: Tiger Balm, Snake Dust, aconite, Pain Begone, Miracle Wort. Others offered services on the spot: painless dentistry, spinal realignment, Chinese herbs brewed to the taste, head massages. Sabina, who had attended the medicine show with John after moving to San Francisco—a must, he'd said, for new residents—recognized several of the participants: Pawnee Bill, The Great Ferndon, Doctor Jekyll, Herman the Healer, Rodney Strongheart.

The din rose as a shill for Dr. Wallmann's Nerve and Brain Salts stood in his red coach—six black horses stamping and snorting—to extol the product. Sabina smiled; John had frequently posed as a drummer for Dr. Wallmann's, and said the salts were nothing more than table salt mixed with borax.

Someone nearby shouted: "The show is on!" A top-hatted magician and his sultry, robed assistant emerged from a striped tent; another show—Indians in dancing regalia—began to compete, the thump of tom-toms drowning out a banjo player. The entertainment quickly ended when the selling began.

Sabina continued to scan the scene before her. The crowd was mostly men; the few women she judged to be of the lower classes by their worn clothing and roughened faces and hands. Not a lady—fancy or fine—in the lot. And no one with a picture hat and unusual pin. However, the woman she sought could have changed her clothing as she herself had. Sabina moved into the crowd.

A snake charmer's flute caught her attention, and she watched the pathetic defanged creature rise haltingly from its shabby basket. She turned away, spied under the wide brim of a battered straw hat. The woman had dark eyes and gray hair—not the person she was looking for.

On a platform at the back of a wagon, a dancer was performing, draped in filmy veils. Unfortunately the veils slipped and fell to the ground, revealing her scarlet long johns. A man with an ostrich-feather-bedecked hat began expounding upon the virtues of Sydney's Cough Syrup, only to fall into a fit of coughing. Sabina glanced at the face under the brim of an old-fashioned bonnet and saw the woman was elderly.

Wide-brimmed hat with bedraggled feathers: a badly scarred young woman whose plight made Sabina flinch. Toque-draped in fading tulle: red hair, and freckles. Another bonnet: white hair and fine wrinkles.

As Sabina was approaching a model of France's infamous guillotine, a cry rang out. She soon saw that the ostrich feathers of the spokesman for Sydney's Cough Syrup had caught fire from one of the torches. A nearby man rushed to throw the hat to the ground and stomp the flames out.

A freak show was starting. The barker urged Sabina to enter the tent and view the dwarf and deformed baby in a bottle. She declined—not at all respectfully.

Extravagant hat with many layers of feathers and a stuffed bird's head protruding at the front: long blonde hair. Temperance speakers, exhibiting jars containing diseased kidneys. No, thank you.

Another bird hat. What *was* the fascination with wearing dead avian creatures on one's head? The woman beneath the brim looked not much healthier than the bird that had died to grace her headpiece.

A barker tried to entice Sabina into a wax display of a hanging. No to that, also.

Worn blue velvet wide-brimmed hat, secured by . . . a Charles Horner hatpin, blue glass overlaid with a gold pattern. Ah! The woman moved through the crowd, head swiveling from side to side.

Sabina waited until her quarry was several yards ahead of her, then followed.

The woman pretended interest in a miraculous

electrified belt filled with cayenne pepper whose purveyor claimed would cure any debilitation. She stopped to listen to the Negro minstrels and clapped appreciatively when their music ended. Considered a temperance pamphlet, but shook her head. Accepted a flyer from the seller of White's Female Complaint Cure.

All the time, as Sabina covertly watched her, the pickpocket's head continued to move from side to side—looking for someone in distress. Someone who she could rob.

Sabina seldom had difficulty controlling her temper. True, it rose swiftly, but just as swiftly it turned from hot outrage to cold resolve. She, too, began looking for someone in distress. Someone who she could save from the woman's thievery.

Before long, she saw him, nearly ten yards away, humped over, leaning on a cane, walking haltingly. She poised to move in, but the woman, who obviously had seen him, too, surprised her by turning the other way.

Another old man, limping, forehead shiny with perspiration in spite of the chill temperature.

The woman passed him by.

Had Sabina been wrong about the pickpocket's method? No, this dip was clever. She was waiting for the ideal victim.

More wandering. More pretending interest in the shows and wares. No indication that the pickpocket had spied her.

In front of the bright red coach belonging to the purveyor of Dr. Wallmann's Nerve and Brain Salts, the woman stopped. She spoke to the vendor, examined the bottle, then shook her head. A crowd had pressed in behind her. She stretched her arms up behind her head, then dropped them, and angled through the people.

And in that moment Sabina knew her method.

She pushed forward into the crowd, keeping her eyes on the blue velvet picture hat. It moved diagonally, toward the Chinese herbalist's wagon. Now, after 10:00 p.m., most of the women had departed, their places taken by Cocktail Route travelers on a postprandial stroll, after which many would visit the establishments of the wicked Barbary Coast. The woman in the blue hat would be there, too, plying her trade upon the unsuspecting—unless Sabina could stop her.

The blue hat now brushed against the shoulder of a tall, blond man clad in an elegant broadloom suit. The perfect victim.

Sabina weaved her way through men who had stopped to hear Rodney Strongheart sing in a loud baritone about how his elixir would keep one's heart beating forever. A few gave her disapproving glances—she should not be here at this hour, and she certainly shouldn't be elbowing them aside.

Sabina continued to use her elbows.

Now she was beside the woman. She reached for

her arm and missed it just as the man in broadloom groaned and clutched his side. Sabina saw the dip's right hand move to his inner pocket; she was quick, and the man's purse was soon in her grasp.

But not soon enough to make her escape.

Sabina grasped the woman's right hand, which held the purse, and pinned the dip's arm behind her back. The pickpocket struggled, and Sabina pulled the arm higher until she cried out, and then was still.

The victim had recovered from his pain. He stared at Sabina, then at the thief. Sabina reached down and wrested the blue-and-gold Charles Horner hatpin from the woman's hand.

"And that," John Quincannon said, "was the last of the Carville Ghost." He looked pleased with himself, sitting at his desk, smiling and stroking his freebooter's beard—a feature that made him appear rakish and dangerous. He fancied himself the world's finest detective and he always preened a bit when he brought an investigation to a successful conclusion. "And," he added, "I have collected the fee. A not inconsiderable twenty-five hundred dollars. I would say that justifies dinner for two at Marchand's and perhaps . . ."

Sabina interrupted his description of his evening's plans for them. "I, too, have collected a handsome fee. From Charles Ackerman."

"Ah, you solved the pickpocketing case."

"Yes." She proceeded to tell him about it, finishing: "I thought the woman . . . Sarah Wilds . . . was preying upon infirm men, perhaps men in gastric distress. It turned out she was stealing from perfectly healthy men, stabbing them in the side with her needle-thin hatpin to distract them while she picked their pockets."

"Needle-thin?" John frowned. "I presented you with a silver-and-coral Charles Horner hatpin on your last birthday. As I recall, it was fairly thick."

"Sarah Wilds had altered hers, so the pin would pass through clothing and flesh, but not cause the victim to bleed much, if at all. Just a painful prick, and she'd withdraw it while reaching for her victim's valuables."

"But the man who died . . . Harry Holbrooke?"

"Henry. The police assume he was unlucky. The pin went in too deeply, punctured an organ, and caused bleeding and an infection. You must remember . . . Sarah Wilds was using the same pin over and over. Think of the bacteria it carried."

John nodded. "Another job well done, my dear. Now, about Marchand's and perhaps . . ."

"I accept your invitation upon one condition."

"And that is?"

"You will pay for your evening from the proceeds of your Carville investigation, and I will pay for mine from my proceeds."

John, as Sabina had known he would, bristled.

"A lady paying her own way on a celebratory evening . . . unthinkable!"

"You had best think about it, because those are my terms."

He sighed—a long exhalation—and scowled fiercely. But as she knew he would, he said: "An evening out with you, my dear, is acceptable under any terms or conditions."

As was an evening out with him.

THE DYING TIME

by Marcia Muller
and Bill Pronzini

MELISSA

Autumn leaves skittered along the narrow main street of the small town in California's gold country. They leaped the high curb, rattled down the board sidewalk, and drifted against the bench where I sat dying.

Was this where it was to end—Murphys, population around 300? A hard, wooden-slatted bench my last resting place in this life? Tricked-up shops and polyester-clad tourists my last sight? What was I doing here, anyway? Traveling aimlessly, as my husband and I had done over the past five years, possessed of more time and money than purposes and enthusiasms.

The pain was growing stronger now; if I had any chance to survive, I had better do something soon. But I felt curiously lethargic and resigned. Even the prospect of a painful death didn't seem to bother me.

It had been a good life up until this past year. I'd accomplished most of the modest things I'd set out to do, had visited most of the places I wanted to see. Of course there were loose ends, but didn't everyone leave a few of those? There was the emptiness of the past few years, but what were a few out of many? And then there were the events of September and my growing suspicions about the terrible way Jake Hollis had died. . . .

I didn't want to think about Jake. That was in the past, over now. All over. As my life soon would be.

Strange. I hadn't expected to feel such detachment at the end. I seemed as little a part of the dying woman on the bench as the leaves that drifted at her feet. They were dying, too, torn by the wind from the trees that had sustained them through the sudden rainstorms of spring, the blistering heat of summer, the first frosts of autumn. Dying like . . .

"What the hell's the matter with you?"

Slowly I looked up. My husband Ray had returned from the used-book shop with a package under his arm. A handsome man yet, blond and tanned and fit, dressed in a new brown cashmere sweater and cords. Handsome as the day I'd met him at the sorority open house twenty-six years ago. A quarter century of marriage, so long that I could scarcely remember a time when he wasn't there. Always there, yet so often absent even when physically present.

I should have sensed that quality even before we were married. The way his eyes kept moving restlessly as he pretended interest in what I was saying. The way he replied with nods and utterances that were mere reaction to my tone of voice, rather than my words' content. But I was twenty years old; what did I know of a man for whom the real world was never quite enough? A man who sought elusive fulfillment in the new and strange and different, as if he might then enter another dimension that would measure up to his expectations.

Nothing had ever measured up. Nothing. Not a stellar career that began with the glimmerings of what the media now called the Information Age and culminated in the sale of the last of three computer software firms he'd founded—a sale unprecedented in financial annals that ensured the security of our children and their heirs for generations to come. The children—Donna and Andrew—certainly hadn't measured up; he'd given them scant attention, and now they had drifted away. There were the various pursuits, all dangerous—flying, mountain climbing, auto racing—and now all discarded. Even the latest passion, skydiving, was a thing of the past. I would be the last to go, the wife who had become nothing more than a good traveling companion.

The Caribbean in winter, when rains soaked northern California. Paris in the springtime. Alaskan cruises to escape the heat of summer in the Napa Valley. African photo safaris, visits to Egypt's pyramids, tours of China and Russia. Hawaii at the holidays when our children and their families failed to return home. We migrated like birds, but insulated from unpleasantness and with fewer surprises.

Until this past month.

"Melissa, I asked you, what's the matter?" Feigned concern turned the fine lines at his eyes' corners to furrows. With an effort I said: "I'm not feeling well."

"I told you you shouldn't have made that chicken pasta for lunch. It's a warm day, and heavy food and wine . . ."

I nodded wearily. It wasn't the pasta or the wine, but there was no point in arguing. The only point was in calling for help, trying to save myself. And I still couldn't seem to care. I was dying, and Ray had poisoned me.

RAY

Melissa didn't want to leave the bench. "It's already too late, isn't it?" she said dully.

"Too late for what?"

"Oh, God, Ray, I can die here as well as anywhere else. It's peaceful here. . . ."

"Die? Don't be silly, you're not going to die."

She squeezed her eyes shut, grimacing, and wouldn't say another word.

I was tempted to let her sit there with her stomach ache and suffer. She could be exasperating sometimes, when she was in one of her moods. She tended to exaggerate and overdramatize situations even at her best, and, whenever she was hurt or upset or angry, she retreated so deeply inside herself that no matter what I did or how hard I tried, I couldn't reach her.

Not that I'd ever been able to get to the core of her, really, except in small ways and for short glimpses. There was just no common ground for us. I live in the real world; I don't believe in anything I can't touch or see or smell. I have strong appetites—sex, food, danger. I take life in both hands and squeeze hard. Melissa is just the opposite. She's a romantic, a sentimentalist; she lives in a fantasy world of dreams and ideals, searching for comforts and fulfillments that I can't give her, that nobody can, because even she doesn't understand exactly what it is she wants out of life. "Little girl lost" is an apt description of her. Dorothy wandering around in some fantastic Oz of her own devising, where everything and everybody is strange and bewildering.

That lost quality was part of what attracted me to her in the beginning. It's very appealing in a beautiful young woman; it makes her more desirable, the chase and catch more exhilarating. Chase and catch weren't enough for me in Melissa's case, though. Before we slept together the first time, I knew I was in love with her. But how can you keep on loving someone you can touch only part of the time, like a ghost who drifts in and out of your life and bed, substantial for a while and then little more than vapor? I don't deal well with frustration or failure, yet that's what Melissa had come to represent.

It was the same for her, I suppose. I'm not what she wants or understands, either. That's why she keeps drifting from one affair to another—looking for someone who's more like she is, who can give her what she wants or thinks she wants. A satisfaction I could always take until recently is that none of the men measured up any more than I have. None until the last one.

Jake Hollis. My good skydiving pal, Jake. He must have measured up. He must've been what she wanted. Otherwise, why would the two of them have plotted to kill me?

She had to have been part of it, much as I hated the thought. It'd been her idea that Jake and I go jumping that day; I remember her suggesting it. And she'd gone along with us, the first time in years she wanted to be in the plane for one of my dives. I don't know why I agreed. I knew by then she was sleeping with Hollis. But murder . . . the possibility never even occurred to me. His hands on my back, clawing at my chute . . . I can still feel them. Trying to rip the pack off so I'd plummet to my death. A few years younger, a little stronger, but not as determined to survive as I'd been. That's the main reason his chute was the one damaged in the struggle, his body the one that plummeted 2,000 feet to shatter on the hard earth.

She didn't cry for him, at least not in front of me. Shock, horror, but no tears. Retreated inside herself to that place no one else can ever go—like the Cheshire cat when it vanished. If she had cried in front of me, I think I would've confronted her then and there. Two weeks now since it happened and I still haven't done it. And I don't know why. This trip to the Sierra foothills, the pretense that everything is reasonably normal between us . . . it's a fool's game. If she and one of her lovers had tried to kill me in the past, I wouldn't have hesitated to accuse her, throw her out, take some sort of revenge. Now . . . I don't know. I'm still hanging on to life with both hands, but the grip isn't as strong as it used to be. Neither are the highs nor the lows, the emotions that once raged in me like torrents. It's as if part of me, or something within me, did die that day, along with Jake Hollis.

I ought to hate her, but I don't. I feel sorry for her.

She was still sitting with her eyes closed, her hands clutched at her middle, her mouth twisted. Typical of her. An upset stomach, and she turns it into high drama.

"Melissa," I said, "we're going back to the lodge. Right now."

She didn't object this time. "All right."

I helped her up, put my arm around her, and led her to the car. People watched us, one or two with concerned expressions or small, approving smiles. Solicitous husband helping unwell wife. The scene was so outwardly caring, loving, that I felt an urge to laugh. But I didn't. There was nothing left to laugh about.

And now my stomach was beginning to bother me. Sharp little cramping pains. Sympathy pains? That was almost funny, too—but not quite.

I helped Melissa into the car and took us away from the watching eyes, away from Murphys. Tom Moore's hunting lodge was eight miles higher up in the mountains—a secluded retreat, a place for lovers. Why had I agreed to come here? Why had Melissa agreed? What was the sense in us getting away alone together, with the end for us so near?

Halfway to the lodge, the cramps grew worse. The pain was stabbing and I was feeling nauseous by the time I reached the turn-off. Beside me, Melissa sat hunched over, holding her stomach, her face pale. Pretending, to throw me off guard? Those thoughts came on the heels of the other one, the one that made me jerk and clench my hands tightly around the wheel.

Christ, what if she'd poisoned me?

MELISSA

In the car on the road leading to our borrowed mountain cabin Ray asked me in what way I wasn't feeling well. Nausea and stomach cramps, I told him, as well as a headache.

"Must be the flu," he said. "I feel the same way, except I've also got chills."

Liar, I thought. This was like no flu I'd ever experienced. "How long have you felt sick?"

"A little while."

Then why had he eaten with apparent enjoyment a huge helping of the chicken pasta I'd fixed for lunch? Why had he suggested we drive into town and then spent so long browsing in the bookshop if he was feeling bad? Faking, of course, so I wouldn't guess the truth. Except that I'd already guessed it.

"How awful for you," I said.

"You're certainly the sympathetic one."

I turned my face to the side window and didn't reply. My cramps were growing worse; the poison was doing its work.

At the rustic wood-and-stone lodge belonging to Tom Moore, his former business partner, Ray pulled the car close to the front steps, jumped out, and rushed up them without waiting for me. By the time I made my way inside, he was in the bathroom off the front hallway, making violent retching sounds. Acting again.

He was a consummate actor, I thought as I went upstairs to the living room and slumped in one of the armchairs in front of the huge fireplace. All those years of high-level business dealings, all those years of pretending interest in and affection for the children and me—they had polished his art. And now he was playing his biggest rôle of all, unaware that his audience of one wasn't the slightest bit fooled.

I leaned my head back against the chair, narrowed my eyes, and looked around. Knotty pine everywhere. God, how I hated knotty pine! Every uncomfortable mountain or lakefront cabin I'd ever stayed in was paneled in the stuff, and now I was going to die surrounded by it.

A violent surge of nausea swept through me; bile rose in my throat. Ray was still in the downstairs bathroom, and I'd never make it upstairs in time, so I rushed to the kitchen and was sick in the sink. Leaning with my hands braced against the countertop, I thought distractedly: *All the work I did cleaning up in here . . . ruined.* Not that Tom would care. The man's become a slob since his poor wife died.

His poor wife died. . . .

That's what they'd be saying about Ray soon. What did he plan to tell people? That I'd been poisoned by accident? Or did he intend to get rid of my body? Claim I'd disappeared? Bury me some place in these woods . . . ?

My stomach contracted again; another cramp, more intense than any pain I'd ever experienced outside of childbirth, left me weak and breathless. And suddenly the apathy I'd felt since Murphys was gone. I didn't want to die this way, in agony. I didn't want to die at all. I'd thought I already had, spiritually, as I'd watched Jake Hollis plummet through the air. But that simply wasn't true. After a moment I felt well enough to move across the room to a little desk with shelves containing cookbooks and other household volumes. The chills Ray had mentioned were starting now. What kind of poison produced chills? Had Ray chosen it because its symptoms mimicked a bad case of the flu? He hadn't wanted me to know I was dying.

Unlike Jake. He'd known in those last few awful minutes.

The scene I'd witnessed from the plane two weeks earlier replayed itself in my mind: Ray and Jake struggling in mid-air, neither chute open. Ray's suddenly blossoming upward, while Jake fell, arms and legs flailing. And when the pilot and I arrived at the airstrip, there was Ray, pretending to be completely broken up over our friend's death. Over and over he repeated: "I just don't know what happened."

And I had kept my silence, even though I knew what had happened—and why.

Jake Hollis was dead. Perhaps the closest person to a friend Ray ever had. My friend, too; I'd turned to him in desperation when I sensed my marriage was finally about to end. Not for sex, as I had to two other men in the past, but for insight into what had brought Ray and me to this point. But although Jake had heard me out through two long lunches and an afternoon of drinks, he could shed no light on the situation. Ray had kept him as much at an arm's length as he had me.

For days after Jake's death I'd felt numb, unable to cry, unable to confront Ray with the fact that I knew what he'd done. I even tried to deny it myself, pretend I hadn't seen the mid-air struggle; it seemed too monstrous an act for the man I'd lived with for a quarter of a century. But then a violent scene from five years before escaped from where I'd buried it in my memory: Ray raging at me, having found out about the second of my two brief affairs. His face red and contorted, his eyes wild, he'd accused me of repeated infidelities throughout our marriage. Berated me for sleeping with a member of his mountain-climbing team. Screamed: "I'll kill him! I swear, on the next climb I'll grab hold of him and pitch him off Denali! If I have to go down with him, I will!"

He hadn't, of course. Instead, he'd spent five years nursing his rage and imagining I was sleeping with every man I met. And when that rage was at a fever pitch, he'd turned it on Jake. Killed his friend because he overheard a phone call between us. Killed him because another so-called friend had told him of seeing Jake and me in intimate conversation in a neighborhood cocktail lounge. I'd denied either when he asked me about them; now I wished I had told him why I'd been talking to Jake.

I laid my aching head on the desk and moaned. Finally the tears that shock had frozen began to flow.

Why did you kill him, Ray?

Why didn't you just kill me?

Ray

Emptying my stomach didn't help much. I still felt sick and shaky when I came out of the downstairs bathroom. This wasn't the flu or any other kind of natural illness; there was no doubt of it now. *Call nine-eleven,* I thought, *ask for medical assistance.* But it would take a while for an ambulance or medevac helicopter to get here from Jackson or Sonora and I could be dead by then.

What kind of poison had she used? If I knew that, there might be something I could take to counteract it. At least I could tell the emergency operator, who could then alert the paramedics.

It was an effort to climb the stairs to the upper floor. Ray Porter, who had climbed mountains, hiked through jungles and across deserts—so damned weak he couldn't mount a dozen steps without streaming sweat and hanging onto the railing with both hands. It enraged me, the idea of dying this way, weak and helpless. Yet the funny thing was, most of the rage was at myself for allowing such a thing to happen.

My fault, as much as Melissa's. I'd driven her into Jake Hollis's arms, the arms of all the others. I'd destroyed her, slowly and surely, with the heat of my passions. And in the process I'd sown the seeds of my own destruction.

But not blaming her or hating her didn't mean I would let her get away with what she'd done. Life was still precious to me, and I wouldn't let go of it without a fight.

She wasn't in the kitchen. She had been, though; as I passed the stove, I smelled a sour odor and saw that she'd thrown up in the sink. My God! Maybe she hadn't been faking in Murphys or on the way up here; maybe she'd poisoned herself, too. Hollis was dead, she couldn't have him, and she didn't want me any more, so what did she have left to live for? It was just like her to concoct a quixotic Shakespearean finish for both of us.

I stumbled into the living room. She wasn't there, either, but I could hear her—low sobbing sounds coming from out on the balcony that ran across the entire rear of the lodge. I almost fell before I reached the open balcony doors; I had to clutch at the glass for support, all but drag myself around the jamb. The weakness and the cramping pain made me even more determined.

Melissa was sitting on one of the redwood chairs, her arms wrapped across her middle, rocking slightly and grimacing. A closed book lay in her lap. A book, for God's sake, at a time like this!

"Melissa."

She stiffened and her head turned toward me. Her eyes were enormous, luminous with pain. In spite of what she'd done, in spite of myself, I experienced a surge of feeling for her—compassion, protectiveness, even tenderness, like suddenly materialized ghosts from the past.

"Why, Ray?" she said. "Why did this have to happen?"

"You know the answer to that better than I do. But it's not too late. I won't let it be too late."

"I don't want to die. I thought I did, for a while, but I don't."

"Neither of us is going to die. I'll call for emergency medical help . . . but I have to know what it was first." She shook her head as if she didn't understand.

"The poison," I said. "What kind of poison?"

"How should I know! Ray, don't torture me any more. . . ."

"Listen to me. It's not too late. An antidote, some kind of emetic . . . what did you use?"

"I didn't . . . I didn't . . ."

I lurched toward her, fell to my knees beside her chair. "How long ago? What kind of poison? How much?"

"Stop it! You know it wasn't me!"

"Melissa . . ."

"You did it. You, you, you!"

I stared at her in disbelief. "That's crazy. I wouldn't do a thing like that to you, to myself. I wouldn't hurt you."

"But if you didn't poison us . . . ?"

"I didn't." Confusion gripped me now; I couldn't seem to think clearly. "And you swear you didn't?"

"I swear!"

"If it wasn't poison, then what . . ." I broke off, staring at the book in her lap, seeing its title for the first time. *Symptoms: The Complete Home Medical Encyclopedia.*

I reached out to it—and the pain came again, a sudden wrenching so violent it brought an involuntary cry from my throat. Gagging, I clutched at Melissa. Felt her hands on me. And then we were clinging to each other, holding tighter than we had in a long, long time.

MELISSA

As Ray kneeled beside my chair and we held each other, I felt something that I'd never felt for him before: compassion. He'd never needed it, never wanted it, and he probably wouldn't now. But a man who had climbed mountains, who had been unafraid to step out into space with only a parachute to depend on—it tore at my heart to see him reduced to this sweating, trembling weakness by . . . what?

He was staring at the home medical encyclopedia I'd found on the shelf above the kitchen desk. Now he raised his eyes to mine and said thickly: "Did you look up our symptoms in there?"

"No, not yet. . . ."

He reached again for the book, but another wave of pain drove him down into a sitting position, forehead against my knees.

"Can't do it," he said. "My eyes . . ."

The admission seemed to rob him of his last strength. Ray had always taken charge, always, in every situation.

A sharp spasm wrenched my stomach. When it eased, I put my hand on the back of his head and said: "I can."

It was a huge volume, and for a moment I couldn't focus on how to use it. Then I realized the first part was a reverse dictionary of symptoms; you looked yours up, and it referred you to the causes described in the second section. I started with the section on nausea and vomiting.

"This doesn't help," I muttered after scanning the entry. Vomiting. . . . Characteristic of nearly all infectious diseases, none of which it was likely we'd both come down with. . . . Wait, here was vomiting coupled with headache. . . .

Ray grabbed onto my calves now, his fingers spasming along with his body. More cramps, worse than what I was experiencing. I gripped his shoulder reassuringly and read on.

Brain tumors, migraine headache, acute glaucoma. . . .

Oh, God, this was no good! I felt the beginnings of panic, took a deep breath, and continued skimming the entry. It told me nothing.

Ray moaned, his face contorted.

I flipped to the front of the book, looking for a table of contents. An encyclopedia of symptoms—wouldn't they expect that a user might be in pain, want answers in a hurry? Why wasn't there . . . ?

Severe pain in the abdomen, nausea, cramps, vomiting. Acute gastritis. . . . Staphylococcus. . . . Botulism. . . . "I've narrowed it down. Hold on."

"What . . . ?"

A strong spasm stiffened me before I could focus clearly on the next page. The chills that followed were intense enough to make my teeth chatter.

"Melissa?"

"I'll be all right in a minute. Are your eyes any better?"

". . . A little."

I fumbled the book toward him. "Look at page three fifty-two, darling. Three fifty-two. . . ."

RAY

Darling. Had I heard that right? She hadn't called me darling, dear, honey, any of the endearments in a long while, even on the rare occasions the past few years when we'd made love. . . .

Another twinge of pain made me grit my teeth, focus on the open book. Page 352. Infected Food, Gastroenteritis. Usually due to eating food that is infected by salmonella bacteria.

Food poisoning. What fools we'd been, each imagining that the other had resorted to arsenic, strychnine, some damned thing. And all along . . .

"Salmonella," I said. "But how did we get it? We haven't eaten anywhere but here the past couple of days."

"The kitchen! You remember how filthy it was when we arrived? I thought I cleaned everything thoroughly, but I must've missed something. . . ."

That damn' plastic cutting board. Bacteria breeds in plastic like that, and I diced the raw chicken on it for our pasta."

Rarely fatal, the book said. But nevertheless a medical alert. Severe cases develop dehydration, kidney failure with urinary suppression, shock. Call physician immediately.

"Nine-eleven," I said. "Can't waste any more time." I tried to push up onto my feet, but I seemed to have no strength in my arms or legs. The entire lower half of my body felt heavy, almost numb from the vomiting and cramping.

"You're too weak."

"No. I've got to make the call. . . ."

"You ate more than I did," Melissa said, "your case is more severe. I feel better now . . . I'll do it." She touched my face. "I'm the strong one right now, darling. Let me be the strong one for once."

I looked up at her through the wetness and the pain. The same Melissa, the same woman I'd married and had children with and lived with for a quarter of a century. And yet she seemed different somehow. Or maybe I was seeing her differently. The little-girl-lost quality was gone; for the first time I saw strength in my wife. Hazily I wondered if it was something new, a courage born of this crisis, or if it had been there all along, hidden or suppressed or just not visible to me for what it was.

I clung to the chair, weak, and watched Melissa stand up, strong, and make her way toward the open doors. And a voice that didn't sound like mine, that almost whimpered like a hurt child's, called after her: "Hurry, baby, hurry. . . ."

MELISSA

Ray had collapsed against the chair when I came back. "They're sending a medevac helicopter," I told him. "We're going to be OK." Then I sank down beside him, pulling an Afghan over both of us. He grasped my hand the way the children used to when I'd comfort them after bad nightmares.

A nightmare, that's what today was.

"Melissa," he said after a moment, "why did you think I poisoned you?"

"It isn't important now." We'd have to talk about it, of course, but later, when we were both stronger. I'd finally have to confront him about Jake. After that . . .

"No, please, I need to know."

". . . After Jake . . . died. . . ."

"Jake? What does his death have to do with this?"

"I was there, Ray. I saw the two of you struggling in mid-air."

His lips twisted and he let go of my hand. "The son-of-a-bitch tried to kill me."

"Jake, kill you? He was your friend. You meant a lot to him."

"He was your lover."

"No, my friend, too. All we ever did when we were alone together was talk about you and why our marriage was dying."

A spasm overcame him, and he made a choking sound. When he recovered, he didn't speak. I felt a coldness in him—anger, too, directed at me. And suddenly I understood.

"Oh, no!" I said. "You think Jake tried to kill you because of me. You think we conspired to get rid of you!"

His pain-dull eyes watched me for a moment. "You didn't plan to kill me? And you weren't sleeping with him?"

"I told you I wasn't. I've slept with exactly two men other than you in my life . . . the last over five years ago. And even if I had been having an affair with Jake, I would never have plotted to hurt you." The tears I'd been controlling started again.

Ray put a shaky hand to my cheek, tried to brush them away. "What've I been thinking? Accusing you over and over. And today . . . I thought you'd decided you couldn't go on without Jake and were going to . . . Christ, what a hideous, twisted imagination I've got!"

"No more than mine. I thought you killed Jake and were faking your illness so I wouldn't realize you'd poisoned me."

He shook his head, grimacing. "You know, this would be funny if it wasn't so . . ."

"Yes."

We sat silently for a while. A distant *thrumming* and *flapping* noise came from beyond the pine-covered hills to the west.

"What about Jake?" Ray asked. "Why did he grab at my chute like that? There has to be a reason." He closed his eyes, probably reliving the horrifying experience. "Oh, God," he said heavily.

"What?"

"Jake taught skydiving, remember. Instructors are trained to notice things that other divers might not. He wasn't trying to kill me . . . he was trying to save my life. He must've seen something that told him my chute wasn't going to open. And he saved me at the expense of himself."

Ray lowered his face into his hands and made a strange sound. At first I couldn't identify it, then I realized he was crying. I'd never seen him shed so much as a single tear.

I peeled his hands away, took his face in both of mine, and kissed him. No words could ease the grief and shame we were feeling. There were not enough words to do that.

RAY

We were both composed again by the time the medevac helicopter arrived. Huddled together under the Afghan, holding hands. We hadn't said much after the revelations about Jake Hollis's death; there was only one issue left to discuss, and neither of us was quite ready to put it into words.

Every time I looked at her now, it was as if twenty-six years had melted away. I felt the same deep stirrings as I'd felt that first night at her sorority's open house. But it wasn't a young woman's vulnerable beauty that attracted me this time, made me feel alive again; it was a mature woman's capacity for giving and understanding. For such a long time I'd seen only the young Melissa whenever I looked at my wife—an illusion that had begun as reality and gradually evolved into pure fantasy. False illusion was what had driven the wedge between us, led to all the problems and foolish misconceptions we'd both had. And not only on my part—on hers, too.

Neither of us knew the other any more.

I wanted to know her again, everything there was to know about this Melissa—but did she feel the same about me? Did she want to know the Ray Porter I'd grown and changed into, with all his flaws and insecurities? I thought I saw the answer in her eyes, but the spasms that continued to rack us both made me unsure.

The helicopter was down finally, its rotors making a hell of a racket on the road out front. The paramedics would be here any minute. I had to get it out into the open now, before there was any more separation.

I squeezed her hand. "Melissa, it's not too late for us, is it? We can start over again, learn to love each other again?"

"I never stopped loving you," she said.

"Nor I you, but I mean . . ."

"I know what you mean. No more misunderstandings between us. No more walls."

"Yes."

"No more dying," she said, and now I was sure of what was in her eyes. "The dying time is over. Now we can start living again."

ABOUT THE AUTHORS

Born and raised in Detroit, Michigan, **Marcia Muller** has been a full-time novelist since 1983. She received her bachelor's degree in English literature and master's degree in journalism from the University of Michigan. Upon graduation she worked for *Sunset* magazine, and then as a freelance writer as well as being a partner in an editorial services firm. She is the author of numerous crime novels, twenty-three of which feature her much-loved San Francisco investigator, Sharon McCone, who made her debut in 1977. Recipient of numerous awards, including the American Mystery Award and the Private Eye Writers of America Shamus Award, in 1993 Muller was presented with the Private Eye Writers of America's Life Achievement Award for her contribution to the genre. Her interest in the Western story stems from her love of history and research. *Time of the Wolves* (Five Star Westerns, 2003) was her first Western story collection.

Bill Pronzini was born in Petaluma, California. His earliest Western fiction was published in *Zane Grey Western Magazine*. His first Western novel was *The Gallows Land* (1983). Although Pronzini has earned an enviable reputation as an author of detective stories, he has continued periodically to write Western novels, most notably perhaps *Starvation Camp* (1984) and *Firewind* (1989) as well as Western short stories, including *Burgade's Crossing* (Five Star Westerns, 2003) and *Quincannon's Game* (Five Star Westerns, 2005), both collections of Quincannon stories. In his Western stories, Pronzini has tended toward narratives that avoid excessive violence and, instead, are character studies in which a person has to deal with personal flaws or learn to live with the consequences of previous actions. As an editor and anthologist, Pronzini has demonstrated both rare *éclat* and reliable good taste in selecting very fine stories by other authors, fiction notable for its human drama and memorable characters. He is married to author Marcia Muller, who has written Western stories as well as detective stories, and occasionally collaborated with her husband on detective novels. They make their home in Petaluma, California.

ADDITIONAL COPYRIGHT INFORMATION

Center Point Publishing
600 Brooks Road ● PO Box 1
Thorndike ME 04986-0001 USA

(207) 568-3717

US & Canada:
1 800 929-9108
www.centerpointlargeprint.com